GALLEGHER

AND OTHER STORIES

RICHARD HARDING DAVIS

1st WORLD LIBRARY Literary Society

Gallegher and Other Stories

Richard Harding Davis

© 1st World Library – Literary Society, 2006
PO Box 2211
Fairfield, IA 52556
www.1stworldlibrary.org
First Edition

LCCN: 2006905733

Softcover ISBN: 1-4218-2162-1
Hardcover ISBN: 1-4218-2062-5
eBook ISBN: 1-4218-2262-8

Purchase *"Gallegher and Other Stories"*
as a traditional bound book at:
www.1stWorldLibrary.org/purchase.asp?ISBN=1-4218-2162-1

1st World Library Literary Society is a nonprofit
organization dedicated to promoting literacy by:

- Creating a free internet library accessible from any computer worldwide.
- Hosting writing competitions and offering book publishing scholarships.

Gallegher and Other Stories
contributed by Tim, Ed & Rodney
in support of
1st World Library Literary Society

TO

MY MOTHER

CONTENTS

GALLEGHER: A NEWSPAPER STORY

We had had so many office-boys before Gallegher came among us that they had begun to lose the characteristics of individuals, and became merged in a composite photograph of small boys, to whom we applied the generic title of "Here, you"; or "You, boy."

We had had sleepy boys, and lazy boys, and bright, "smart" boys, who became so familiar on so short an acquaintance that we were forced to part with them to save our own self-respect.

They generally graduated into district-messenger boys, and occasionally returned to us in blue coats with nickel-plated buttons, and patronized us.

But Gallegher was something different from anything we had experienced before. Gallegher was short and broad in build, with a solid, muscular broadness, and not a fat and dumpy shortness. He wore perpetually on his face a happy and knowing smile, as if you and the world in general were not impressing him as seriously as you thought you were, and his eyes, which were very black and very bright, snapped intelligently at you like those of a little black-and-tan terrier.

All Gallegher knew had been learnt on the streets; not a very good school in itself, but one that turns out very knowing scholars. And Gallegher had attended both morning and evening sessions. He could not tell you who the Pilgrim Fathers were, nor could he name the thirteen original States, but he knew all the officers of the twenty-second police district by name, and he could distinguish the clang of a fire-engine's gong from that of a patrol-wagon or an ambulance fully two blocks distant. It was Gallegher who rang the alarm when the Woolwich Mills caught fire, while the officer on the beat was asleep, and it was Gallegher who led the "Black Diamonds" against the "Wharf Rats," when they used to stone each other to their hearts' content on the coal-wharves of Richmond.

I am afraid, now that I see these facts written down, that Gallegher was not a reputable character; but he was so very young and so very old for his years that we all liked him very much nevertheless. He lived in the extreme northern part of Philadelphia, where the cotton-and woollen-mills run down to the river, and how he ever got home after leaving the *Press* building at two in the morning, was one of the mysteries of the office. Sometimes he caught a night car, and sometimes he walked all the way, arriving at the little house, where his mother and himself lived alone, at four in the morning. Occasionally he was given a ride on an early milk-cart, or on one of the newspaper delivery wagons, with its high piles of papers still damp and sticky from the press. He knew several drivers of "night hawks" - those cabs that prowl the streets at night looking for belated passengers - and when it was a very cold morning he would not go home at all, but would crawl into one of these cabs and sleep, curled up on the cushions, until daylight.

Besides being quick and cheerful, Gallegher possessed

a power of amusing the *Press's* young men to a degree seldom attained by the ordinary mortal. His clog-dancing on the city editor's desk, when that gentleman was up-stairs fighting for two more columns of space, was always a source of innocent joy to us, and his imitations of the comedians of the variety halls delighted even the dramatic critic, from whom the comedians themselves failed to force a smile.

But Gallegher's chief characteristic was his love for that element of news generically classed as "crime." Not that he ever did anything criminal himself. On the contrary, his was rather the work of the criminal specialist, and his morbid interest in the doings of all queer characters, his knowledge of their methods, their present whereabouts, and their past deeds of transgression often rendered him a valuable ally to our police reporter, whose daily feuilletons were the only portion of the paper Gallegher deigned to read.

In Gallegher the detective element was abnormally developed. He had shown this on several occasions, and to excellent purpose.

Once the paper had sent him into a Home for Destitute Orphans which was believed to be grievously mismanaged, and Gallegher, while playing the part of a destitute orphan, kept his eyes open to what was going on around him so faithfully that the story he told of the treatment meted out to the real orphans was sufficient to rescue the unhappy little wretches from the individual who had them in charge, and to have the individual himself sent to jail.

Gallegher's knowledge of the aliases, terms of imprisonment, and various misdoings of the leading criminals in Philadelphia was almost as thorough as that of the chief of police himself, and he could tell to an hour when "Dutchy Mack" was to be let out of prison, and could identify at a glance "Dick Oxford, confidence man," as "Gentleman Dan, petty thief."

There were, at this time, only two pieces of news in any of the papers. The least important of the two was the big fight between the Champion of the United States and the Would-be Champion, arranged to take place near Philadelphia; the second was the Burrbank murder, which was filling space in newspapers all over the world, from New York to Bombay.

Richard F. Burrbank was one of the most prominent of New York's railroad lawyers; he was also, as a matter of course, an owner of much railroad stock, and a very wealthy man. He had been spoken of as a political possibility for many high offices, and, as the counsel for a great railroad, was known even further than the great railroad itself had stretched its system.

At six o'clock one morning he was found by his butler lying at the foot of the hall stairs with two pistol wounds above his heart. He was quite dead. His safe, to which only he and his secretary had the keys, was found open, and $200,000 in bonds, stocks, and money, which had been placed there only the night before, was found missing. The secretary was missing also. His name was Stephen S. Hade, and his name and his description had been telegraphed and cabled to all parts of the world. There was enough circumstantial evidence to show, beyond any question or possibility of mistake, that he was the murderer.

It made an enormous amount of talk, and unhappy

individuals were being arrested all over the country, and sent on to New York for identification. Three had been arrested at Liverpool, and one man just as he landed at Sydney, Australia. But so far the murderer had escaped.

We were all talking about it one night, as everybody else was all over the country, in the local room, and the city editor said it was worth a fortune to any one who chanced to run across Hade and succeeded in handing him over to the police. Some of us thought Hade had taken passage from some one of the smaller seaports, and others were of the opinion that he had buried himself in some cheap lodging-house in New York, or in one of the smaller towns in New Jersey.

"I shouldn't be surprised to meet him out walking, right here in Philadelphia," said one of the staff. "He'll be disguised, of course, but you could always tell him by the absence of the trigger finger on his right hand. It's missing, you know; shot off when he was a boy."

"You want to look for a man dressed like a tough," said the city editor; "for as this fellow is to all appearances a gentleman, he will try to look as little like a gentleman as possible."

"No, he won't," said Gallegher, with that calm impertinence that made him dear to us. "He'll dress just like a gentleman. Toughs don't wear gloves, and you see he's got to wear 'em. The first thing he thought of after doing for Burrbank was of that gone finger, and how he was to hide it. He stuffed the finger of that glove with cotton so's to make it look like a whole finger, and the first time he takes off that glove they've got him - see, and he knows it. So what youse want to do is to look for a man with gloves on. I've been a-doing it for two weeks now, and I can tell you it's hard work, for everybody wears gloves this kind of weather. But if you look long enough you'll find him. And when you think it's him, go up to him and hold out your hand in a friendly way, like a bunco-steerer, and shake his hand; and if you feel that his forefinger ain't real flesh, but just wadded cotton, then grip to it with your right and grab his throat with your left, and holler for help."

There was an appreciative pause.

"I see, gentlemen," said the city editor, dryly, "that Gallegher's reasoning has impressed you; and I also see that before the week is out all of my young men will be under bonds for assaulting innocent pedestrians whose only offence is that they wear gloves in midwinter."

It was about a week after this that Detective Hefflefinger, of Inspector Byrnes's staff, came over to Philadelphia after a burglar, of whose whereabouts he had been misinformed by telegraph. He brought the warrant, requisition, and other necessary papers with him, but the burglar had flown. One of our reporters had worked on a New York paper, and knew Hefflefinger, and the detective came to the office to see if he could help him in his so far unsuccessful search.

He gave Gallegher his card, and after Gallegher had read it, and had discovered who the visitor was, he became so demoralized that he was absolutely useless.

"One of Byrnes's men" was a much more awe-inspiring individual to Gallegher than a member of the

Cabinet. He accordingly seized his hat and overcoat, and leaving his duties to be looked after by others, hastened out after the object of his admiration, who found his suggestions and knowledge of the city so valuable, and his company so entertaining, that they became very intimate, and spent the rest of the day together.

In the meanwhile the managing editor had instructed his subordinates to inform Gallegher, when he condescended to return, that his services were no longer needed. Gallegher had played truant once too often. Unconscious of this, he remained with his new friend until late the same evening, and started the next afternoon toward the *Press* office.

As I have said, Gallegher lived in the most distant part of the city, not many minutes' walk from the Kensington railroad station, where trains ran into the suburbs and on to New York.

It was in front of this station that a smoothly shaven, well-dressed man brushed past Gallegher and hurried up the steps to the ticket office.

He held a walking-stick in his right hand, and Gallegher, who now patiently scrutinized the hands of every one who wore gloves, saw that while three fingers of the man's hand were closed around the cane, the fourth stood out in almost a straight line with his palm.

Gallegher stopped with a gasp and with a trembling all over his little body, and his brain asked with a throb if it could be possible. But possibilities and probabilities were to be discovered later. Now was the time for action.

He was after the man in a moment, hanging at his heels and his eyes moist with excitement. He heard the man ask for a ticket to Torresdale, a little station just outside of Philadelphia, and when he was out of hearing, but not out of sight, purchased one for the same place.

The stranger went into the smoking-car, and seated himself at one end toward the door. Gallegher took his place at the opposite end.

He was trembling all over, and suffered from a slight feeling of nausea. He guessed it came from fright, not of any bodily harm that might come to him, but at the probability of failure in his adventure and of its most momentous possibilities.

The stranger pulled his coat collar up around his ears, hiding the lower portion of his face, but not concealing the resemblance in his troubled eyes and close-shut lips to the likenesses of the murderer Hade.

They reached Torresdale in half an hour, and the stranger, alighting quickly, struck off at a rapid pace down the country road leading to the station.

Gallegher gave him a hundred yards' start, and then followed slowly after. The road ran between fields and past a few frame-houses set far from the road in kitchen gardens.

Once or twice the man looked back over his shoulder, but he saw only a dreary length of road with a small boy splashing through the slush in the midst of it and stopping every now and again to throw snowballs at belated sparrows.

Richard Harding Davis

After a ten minutes' walk the stranger turned into a side road which led to only one place, the Eagle Inn, an old roadside hostelry known now as the headquarters for pothunters from the Philadelphia game market and the battle-ground of many a cock-fight.

Gallegher knew the place well. He and his young companions had often stopped there when out chestnutting on holidays in the autumn.

The son of the man who kept it had often accompanied them on their excursions, and though the boys of the city streets considered him a dumb lout, they respected him somewhat owing to his inside knowledge of dog and cock-fights.

The stranger entered the inn at a side door, and Gallegher, reaching it a few minutes later, let him go for the time being, and set about finding his occasional playmate, young Keppler.

Keppler's offspring was found in the wood-shed.

"'Tain't hard to guess what brings you out here," said the tavern-keeper's son, with a grin; "it's the fight."

"What fight?" asked Gallegher, unguardedly.

"What fight? Why, *the* fight," returned his companion, with the slow contempt of superior knowledge. "It's to come off here to-night. You knew that as well as me; anyway your sportin' editor knows it. He got the tip last night, but that won't help you any. You needn't think there's any chance of your getting a peep at it. Why, tickets is two hundred and fifty apiece!"

"Whew!" whistled Gallegher, "where's it to be?"

"In the barn," whispered Keppler. "I helped 'em fix the ropes this morning, I did."

"Gosh, but you're in luck," exclaimed Gallegher, with flattering envy. "Couldn't I jest get a peep at it?"

"Maybe," said the gratified Keppler. "There's a winder with a wooden shutter at the back of the barn. You can get in by it, if you have some one to boost you up to the sill."

"Sa-a-y," drawled Gallegher, as if something had but just that moment reminded him. "Who's that gent who come down the road just a bit ahead of me - him with the cape-coat! Has he got anything to do with the fight?"

"Him?" repeated Keppler in tones of sincere disgust. "No-oh, he ain't no sport. He's queer, Dad thinks. He come here one day last week about ten in the morning, said his doctor told him to go out 'en the country for his health. He's stuck up and citified, and wears gloves, and takes his meals private in his room, and all that sort of ruck. They was saying in the saloon last night that they thought he was hiding from something, and Dad, just to try him, asks him last night if he was coming to see the fight. He looked sort of scared, and said he didn't want to see no fight. And then Dad says, 'I guess you mean you don't want no fighters to see you.' Dad didn't mean no harm by it, just passed it as a joke; but Mr. Carleton, as he calls himself, got white as a ghost an' says, 'I'll go to the fight willing enough,' and begins to laugh and joke. And this morning he went right into the bar-room, where all the sports were setting, and said he was going into town to see some friends; and as he starts off he laughs an' says, 'This don't look as if I was afraid of seeing people, does it?' but Dad says it was just bluff that made him do it, and Dad thinks that if he hadn't said what he did, this Mr. Carleton wouldn't have left his room at all."

Gallegher had got all he wanted, and much more than he had hoped for - so much more that his walk back to the station was in the nature of a triumphal march.

He had twenty minutes to wait for the next train, and it seemed an hour. While waiting he sent a telegram to Hefflefinger at his hotel. It read: "Your man is near the Torresdale station, on Pennsylvania Railroad; take cab, and meet me at station. Wait until I come. GALLEGHER."

With the exception of one at midnight, no other train stopped at Torresdale that evening, hence the direction to take a cab.

The train to the city seemed to Gallegher to drag itself by inches. It stopped and backed at purposeless intervals, waited for an express to precede it, and dallied at stations, and when, at last, it reached the terminus, Gallegher was out before it had stopped and was in the cab and off on his way to the home of the sporting editor.

The sporting editor was at dinner and came out in the hall to see him, with his napkin in his hand. Gallegher explained breathlessly that he had located the murderer for whom the police of two continents were looking, and that he believed, in order to quiet the suspicions of the people with whom he was hiding, that he would be present at the fight that night.

The sporting editor led Gallegher into his library and shut the door. "Now," he said, "go over all that again."

Gallegher went over it again in detail, and added how he had sent for Hefflefinger to make the arrest in order that it might be kept from the knowledge of the local police and from the Philadelphia reporters.

"What I want Hefflefinger to do is to arrest Hade with the warrant he has for the burglar," explained Gallegher; "and to take him on to New York on the owl train that passes Torresdale at one. It don't get to Jersey City until four o'clock, one hour after the morning papers go to press. Of course, we must fix Hefflefinger so's he'll keep quiet and not tell who his prisoner really is."

The sporting editor reached his hand out to pat Gallegher on the head, but changed his mind and shook hands with him instead.

"My boy," he said, "you are an infant phenomenon. If I can pull the rest of this thing off to-night it will mean the $5,000 reward and fame galore for you and the paper. Now, I'm going to write a note to the managing editor, and you can take it around to him and tell him what you've done and what I am going to do, and he'll take you back on the paper and raise your salary. Perhaps you didn't know you've been discharged?"

"Do you think you ain't a-going to take me with you?" demanded Gallegher.

"Why, certainly not. Why should I? It all lies with the

detective and myself now. You've done your share, and done it well. If the man's caught, the reward's yours. But you'd only be in the way now. You'd better go to the office and make your peace with the chief."

"If the paper can get along without me, I can get along without the old paper," said Gallegher, hotly. "And if I ain't a-going with you, you ain't neither, for I know where Hefflefinger is to be, and you don't, and I won't tell you."

"Oh, very well, very well," replied the sporting editor, weakly capitulating. "I'll send the note by a messenger; only mind, if you lose your place, don't blame me."

Gallegher wondered how this man could value a week's salary against the excitement of seeing a noted criminal run down, and of getting the news to the paper, and to that one paper alone.

From that moment the sporting editor sank in Gallegher's estimation.

Mr. Dwyer sat down at his desk and scribbled off the following note:

> "I have received reliable information that Hade, the Burrbank murderer, will be present at the fight to-night. We have arranged it so that he will be arrested quietly and in such a manner that the fact may be kept from all other papers. I need not point out to you that this will be the most important piece of news in the country to-morrow.
>
> "Yours, etc., MICHAEL E. DWYER."

The sporting editor stepped into the waiting cab, while Gallegher whispered the directions to the driver. He was told to go first to a district-messenger office, and from there up to the Ridge Avenue Road, out Broad Street, and on to the old Eagle Inn, near Torresdale. It was a miserable night. The rain and snow were falling together, and freezing as they fell. The sporting editor got out to send his message to the *Press* office, and then lighting a cigar, and turning up the collar of his great-coat, curled up in the corner of the cab.

"Wake me when we get there, Gallegher," he said. He knew he had a long ride, and much rapid work before him, and he was preparing for the strain.

To Gallegher the idea of going to sleep seemed almost criminal. From the dark corner of the cab his eyes shone with excitement, and with the awful joy of anticipation. He glanced every now and then to where the sporting editor's cigar shone in the darkness, and watched it as it gradually burnt more dimly and went out. The lights in the shop windows threw a broad glare across the ice on the pavements, and the lights from the lamp-posts tossed the distorted shadow of the cab, and the horse, and the motionless driver, sometimes before and sometimes behind them.

After half an hour Gallegher slipped down to the bottom of the cab and dragged out a lap-robe, in which he wrapped himself. It was growing colder, and the damp, keen wind swept in through the cracks until the window-frames and woodwork were cold to the touch.

An hour passed, and the cab was still moving more slowly over the rough surface of partly paved streets, and by single rows of new houses standing at different angles to each other in fields covered with ash-heaps and brick-kilns. Here and there the gaudy lights of a drug-store, and the forerunner of suburban civilization, shone from the end of a new block of houses, and the rubber cape of an occasional policeman showed in the light of the lamp-post that he hugged for comfort.

Then even the houses disappeared, and the cab dragged its way between truck farms, with desolate-looking glass-covered beds, and pools of water, half-caked with ice, and bare trees, and interminable fences.

Once or twice the cab stopped altogether, and Gallegher could hear the driver swearing to himself, or at the horse, or the roads. At last they drew up before the station at Torresdale. It was quite deserted, and only a single light cut a swath in the darkness and showed a portion of the platform, the ties, and the rails glistening in the rain. They walked twice past the light before a figure stepped out of the shadow and greeted them cautiously.

"I am Mr. Dwyer, of the *Press*," said the sporting editor, briskly. "You've heard of me, perhaps. Well, there shouldn't be any difficulty in our making a deal, should there? This boy here has found Hade, and we have reason to believe he will be among the spectators at the fight to-night. We want you to arrest him quietly, and as secretly as possible. You can do it with your papers and your badge easily enough. We want you to pretend that you believe he is this burglar you came over after. If you will do this, and take him away without any one so much as suspecting who he really is, and on the train that passes here at 1.20 for New York, we will give you $500 out of the $5,000 reward. If, however, one other paper, either in New York or

Philadelphia, or anywhere else, knows of the arrest, you won't get a cent. Now, what do you say?"

The detective had a great deal to say. He wasn't at all sure the man Gallegher suspected was Hade; he feared he might get himself into trouble by making a false arrest, and if it should be the man, he was afraid the local police would interfere.

"We've no time to argue or debate this matter," said Dwyer, warmly. "We agree to point Hade out to you in the crowd. After the fight is over you arrest him as we have directed, and you get the money and the credit of the arrest. If you don't like this, I will arrest the man myself, and have him driven to town, with a pistol for a warrant."

Hefflefinger considered in silence and then agreed unconditionally. "As you say, Mr. Dwyer," he returned. "I've heard of you for a thoroughbred sport. I know you'll do what you say you'll do; and as for me I'll do what you say and just as you say, and it's a very pretty piece of work as it stands."

They all stepped back into the cab, and then it was that they were met by a fresh difficulty, how to get the detective into the barn where the fight was to take place, for neither of the two men had $250 to pay for his admittance.

But this was overcome when Gallegher remembered the window of which young Keppler had told him.

In the event of Hade's losing courage and not daring to show himself in the crowd around the ring, it was agreed that Dwyer should come to the barn and warn

Richard Harding Davis

Hefflefinger; but if he should come, Dwyer was merely to keep near him and to signify by a prearranged gesture which one of the crowd he was.

They drew up before a great black shadow of a house, dark, forbidding, and apparently deserted. But at the sound of the wheels on the gravel the door opened, letting out a stream of warm, cheerful light, and a man's voice said, "Put out those lights. Don't youse know no better than that?" This was Keppler, and he welcomed Mr. Dwyer with effusive courtesy.

The two men showed in the stream of light, and the door closed on them, leaving the house as it was at first, black and silent, save for the dripping of the rain and snow from the eaves.

The detective and Gallegher put out the cab's lamps and led the horse toward a long, low shed in the rear of the yard, which they now noticed was almost filled with teams of many different makes, from the Hobson's choice of a livery stable to the brougham of the man about town.

"No," said Gallegher, as the cabman stopped to hitch the horse beside the others, "we want it nearest that lower gate. When we newspaper men leave this place we'll leave it in a hurry, and the man who is nearest town is likely to get there first. You won't be a-following of no hearse when you make your return trip."

Gallegher tied the horse to the very gate-post itself, leaving the gate open and allowing a clear road and a flying start for the prospective race to Newspaper Row.

The driver disappeared under the shelter of the porch, and Gallegher and the detective moved off cautiously to the rear of the barn. "This must be the window," said Hefflefinger, pointing to a broad wooden shutter some feet from the ground.

"Just you give me a boost once, and I'll get that open in a jiffy," said Gallegher.

The detective placed his hands on his knees, and Gallegher stood upon his shoulders, and with the blade of his knife lifted the wooden button that fastened the window on the inside, and pulled the shutter open.

Then he put one leg inside over the sill, and leaning down helped to draw his fellow-conspirator up to a level with the window. "I feel just like I was burglarizing a house," chuckled Gallegher, as he dropped noiselessly to the floor below and refastened the shutter. The barn was a large one, with a row of stalls on either side in which horses and cows were dozing. There was a haymow over each row of stalls, and at one end of the barn a number of fence-rails had been thrown across from one mow to the other. These rails were covered with hay.

In the middle of the floor was the ring. It was not really a ring, but a square, with wooden posts at its four corners through which ran a heavy rope. The space inclosed by the rope was covered with sawdust.

Gallegher could not resist stepping into the ring, and after stamping the sawdust once or twice, as if to assure himself that he was really there, began dancing around it, and indulging in such a remarkable series of fistic manoeuvres with an imaginary adversary that the

Richard Harding Davis

unimaginative detective precipitately backed into a corner of the barn.

"Now, then," said Gallegher, having apparently vanquished his foe, "you come with me." His companion followed quickly as Gallegher climbed to one of the hay-mows, and crawling carefully out on the fence-rail, stretched himself at full length, face downward. In this position, by moving the straw a little, he could look down, without being himself seen, upon the heads of whomsoever stood below. "This is better'n a private box, ain't it?" said Gallegher.

The boy from the newspaper office and the detective lay there in silence, biting at straws and tossing anxiously on their comfortable bed.

It seemed fully two hours before they came. Gallegher had listened without breathing, and with every muscle on a strain, at least a dozen times, when some movement in the yard had led him to believe that they were at the door. And he had numerous doubts and fears. Sometimes it was that the police had learnt of the fight, and had raided Keppler's in his absence, and again it was that the fight had been postponed, or, worst of all, that it would be put off until so late that Mr. Dwyer could not get back in time for the last edition of the paper. Their coming, when at last they came, was heralded by an advance-guard of two sporting men, who stationed themselves at either side of the big door.

"Hurry up, now, gents," one of the men said with a shiver, "don't keep this door open no longer'n is needful."

It was not a very large crowd, but it was wonderfully well selected. It ran, in the majority of its component parts, to heavy white coats with pearl buttons. The white coats were shouldered by long blue coats with astrakhan fur trimmings, the wearers of which preserved a cliqueness not remarkable when one considers that they believed every one else present to be either a crook or a prize-fighter.

There were well-fed, well-groomed club-men and brokers in the crowd, a politician or two, a popular comedian with his manager, amateur boxers from the athletic clubs, and quiet, close-mouthed sporting men from every city in the country. Their names if printed in the papers would have been as familiar as the types of the papers themselves.

And among these men, whose only thought was of the brutal sport to come, was Hade, with Dwyer standing at ease at his shoulder, - Hade, white, and visibly in deep anxiety, hiding his pale face beneath a cloth travelling-cap, and with his chin muffled in a woollen scarf. He had dared to come because he feared his danger from the already suspicious Keppler was less than if he stayed away. And so he was there, hovering restlessly on the border of the crowd, feeling his danger and sick with fear.

When Hefflefinger first saw him he started up on his hands and elbows and made a movement forward as if he would leap down then and there and carry off his prisoner single-handed.

"Lie down," growled Gallegher; "an officer of any sort wouldn't live three minutes in that crowd."

The detective drew back slowly and buried himself again in the straw, but never once through the long fight which followed did his eyes leave the person of the murderer. The newspaper men took their places in the foremost row close around the ring, and kept looking at their watches and begging the master of ceremonies to "shake it up, do."

There was a great deal of betting, and all of the men handled the great roll of bills they wagered with a flippant recklessness which could only be accounted for in Gallegher's mind by temporary mental derangement. Some one pulled a box out into the ring and the master of ceremonies mounted it, and pointed out in forcible language that as they were almost all already under bonds to keep the peace, it behooved all to curb their excitement and to maintain a severe silence, unless they wanted to bring the police upon them and have themselves "sent down" for a year or two.

Then two very disreputable-looking persons tossed their respective principals' high hats into the ring, and the crowd, recognizing in this relic of the days when brave knights threw down their gauntlets in the lists as only a sign that the fight was about to begin, cheered tumultuously.

This was followed by a sudden surging forward, and a mutter of admiration much more flattering than the cheers had been, when the principals followed their hats, and slipping out of their great-coats, stood forth in all the physical beauty of the perfect brute.

Their pink skin was as soft and healthy looking as a baby's, and glowed in the lights of the lanterns like tinted ivory, and underneath this silken covering the great biceps and muscles moved in and out and looked like the coils of a snake around the branch of a tree.

Gentleman and blackguard shouldered each other for a nearer view; the coachmen, whose metal buttons were unpleasantly suggestive of police, put their hands, in the excitement of the moment, on the shoulders of their masters; the perspiration stood out in great drops on the foreheads of the backers, and the newspaper men bit somewhat nervously at the ends of their pencils.

And in the stalls the cows munched contentedly at their cuds and gazed with gentle curiosity at their two fellow-brutes, who stood waiting the signal to fall upon, and kill each other if need be, for the delectation of their brothers.

"Take your places," commanded the master of ceremonies.

In the moment in which the two men faced each other the crowd became so still that, save for the beating of the rain upon the shingled roof and the stamping of a horse in one of the stalls, the place was as silent as a church.

"Time," shouted the master of ceremonies.

The two men sprang into a posture of defence, which was lost as quickly as it was taken, one great arm shot out like a piston-rod; there was the sound of bare fists beating on naked flesh; there was an exultant indrawn gasp of savage pleasure and relief from the crowd, and the great fight had begun.

How the fortunes of war rose and fell, and changed and

Richard Harding Davis

rechanged that night, is an old story to those who listen to such stories; and those who do not will be glad to be spared the telling of it. It was, they say, one of the bitterest fights between two men that this country has ever known.

But all that is of interest here is that after an hour of this desperate brutal business the champion ceased to be the favorite; the man whom he had taunted and bullied, and for whom the public had but little sympathy, was proving himself a likely winner, and under his cruel blows, as sharp and clean as those from a cutlass, his opponent was rapidly giving way.

The men about the ropes were past all control now; they drowned Keppler's petitions for silence with oaths and in inarticulate shouts of anger, as if the blows had fallen upon them, and in mad rejoicings. They swept from one end of the ring to the other, with every muscle leaping in unison with those of the man they favored, and when a New York correspondent muttered over his shoulder that this would be the biggest sporting surprise since the Heenan-Sayers fight, Mr. Dwyer nodded his head sympathetically in assent.

In the excitement and tumult it is doubtful if any heard the three quickly repeated blows that fell heavily from the outside upon the big doors of the barn. If they did, it was already too late to mend matters, for the door fell, torn from its hinges, and as it fell a captain of police sprang into the light from out of the storm, with his lieutenants and their men crowding close at his shoulder.

In the panic and stampede that followed, several of the

men stood as helplessly immovable as though they had seen a ghost; others made a mad rush into the arms of the officers and were beaten back against the ropes of the ring; others dived headlong into the stalls, among the horses and cattle, and still others shoved the rolls of money they held into the hands of the police and begged like children to be allowed to escape.

The instant the door fell and the raid was declared Hefflefinger slipped over the cross rails on which he had been lying, hung for an instant by his hands, and then dropped into the centre of the fighting mob on the floor. He was out of it in an instant with the agility of a pickpocket, was across the room and at Hade's throat like a dog. The murderer, for the moment, was the calmer man of the two.

"Here," he panted, "hands off, now. There's no need for all this violence. There's no great harm in looking at a fight, is there? There's a hundred-dollar bill in my right hand; take it and let me slip out of this. No one is looking. Here."

But the detective only held him the closer.

"I want you for burglary," he whispered under his breath. "You've got to come with me now, and quick. The less fuss you make, the better for both of us. If you don't know who I am, you can feel my badge under my coat there. I've got the authority. It's all regular, and when we're out of this d - d row I'll show you the papers."

He took one hand from Hade's throat and pulled a pair of handcuffs from his pocket.

Richard Harding Davis

"It's a mistake. This is an outrage," gasped the murderer, white and trembling, but dreadfully alive and desperate for his liberty. "Let me go, I tell you! Take your hands off of me! Do I look like a burglar, you fool?"

"I know who you look like," whispered the detective, with his face close to the face of his prisoner. "Now, will you go easy as a burglar, or shall I tell these men who you are and what I *do* want you for? Shall I call out your real name or not? Shall I tell them? Quick, speak up; shall I?"

There was something so exultant - something so unnecessarily savage in the officer's face that the man he held saw that the detective knew him for what he really was, and the hands that had held his throat slipped down around his shoulders, or he would have fallen. The man's eyes opened and closed again, and he swayed weakly backward and forward, and choked as if his throat were dry and burning. Even to such a hardened connoisseur in crime as Gallegher, who stood closely by, drinking it in, there was something so abject in the man's terror that he regarded him with what was almost a touch of pity.

"For God's sake," Hade begged, "let me go. Come with me to my room and I'll give you half the money. I'll divide with you fairly. We can both get away. There's a fortune for both of us there. We both can get away. You'll be rich for life. Do you understand - for life!"

But the detective, to his credit, only shut his lips the tighter.

"That's enough," he whispered, in return. "That's more

than I expected. You've sentenced yourself already. Come!"

Two officers in uniform barred their exit at the door, but Hefflefinger smiled easily and showed his badge.

"One of Byrnes's men," he said, in explanation; "came over expressly to take this chap. He's a burglar; 'Arlie' Lane, *alias* Carleton. I've shown the papers to the captain. It's all regular. I'm just going to get his traps at the hotel and walk him over to the station. I guess we'll push right on to New York to-night."

The officers nodded and smiled their admiration for the representative of what is, perhaps, the best detective force in the world, and let him pass.

Then Hefflefinger turned and spoke to Gallegher, who still stood as watchful as a dog at his side. "I'm going to his room to get the bonds and stuff," he whispered; "then I'll march him to the station and take that train. I've done my share; don't forget yours!"

"Oh, you'll get your money right enough," said Gallegher. "And, sa-ay," he added, with the appreciative nod of an expert, "do you know, you did it rather well."

Mr. Dwyer had been writing while the raid was settling down, as he had been writing while waiting for the fight to begin. Now he walked over to where the other correspondents stood in angry conclave.

The newspaper men had informed the officers who hemmed them in that they represented the principal papers of the country, and were expostulating vigorously with the captain, who had planned the raid, and who declared they were under arrest.

"Don't be an ass, Scott," said Mr. Dwyer, who was too excited to be polite or politic. "You know our being here isn't a matter of choice. We came here on business, as you did, and you've no right to hold us."

"If we don't get our stuff on the wire at once," protested a New York man, "we'll be too late for to-morrow's paper, and -"

Captain Scott said he did not care a profanely small amount for to-morrow's paper, and that all he knew was that to the station-house the newspaper men would go. There they would have a hearing, and if the magistrate chose to let them off, that was the magistrate's business, but that his duty was to take them into custody.

"But then it will be too late, don't you understand?" shouted Mr. Dwyer. "You've got to let us go *now,* at once."

"I can't do it, Mr. Dwyer," said the captain, "and that's all there is to it. Why, haven't I just sent the president of the Junior Republican Club to the patrol-wagon, the man that put this coat on me, and do you think I can let you fellows go after that? You were all put under bonds to keep the peace not three days ago, and here you're at it - fighting like badgers. It's worth my place to let one of you off."

What Mr. Dwyer said next was so uncomplimentary to the gallant Captain Scott that that overwrought individual seized the sporting editor by the shoulder, and shoved him into the hands of two of his men.

This was more than the distinguished Mr. Dwyer could brook, and he excitedly raised his hand in resistance. But before he had time to do anything foolish his wrist was gripped by one strong, little hand, and he was conscious that another was picking the pocket of his great-coat.

He slapped his hands to his sides, and looking down, saw Gallegher standing close behind him and holding him by the wrist. Mr. Dwyer had forgotten the boy's existence, and would have spoken sharply if something in Gallegher's innocent eyes had not stopped him.

Gallegher's hand was still in that pocket, in which Mr. Dwyer had shoved his note-book filled with what he had written of Gallegher's work and Hade's final capture, and with a running descriptive account of the fight. With his eyes fixed on Mr. Dwyer, Gallegher drew it out, and with a quick movement shoved it inside his waistcoat. Mr. Dwyer gave a nod of comprehension. Then glancing at his two guardsmen, and finding that they were still interested in the wordy battle of the correspondents with their chief, and had seen nothing, he stooped and whispered to Gallegher: "The forms are locked at twenty minutes to three. If you don't get there by that time it will be of no use, but if you're on time you'll beat the town - and the country too."

Gallegher's eyes flashed significantly, and nodding his head to show he understood, started boldly on a run toward the door. But the officers who guarded it brought him to an abrupt halt, and, much to Mr. Dwyer's astonishment, drew from him what was apparently a torrent of tears.

"Let me go to me father. I want me father," the boy shrieked, hysterically. "They've 'rested father. Oh, daddy, daddy. They're a-goin' to take you to prison."

"Who is your father, sonny?" asked one of the guardians of the gate.

"Keppler's me father," sobbed Gallegher. "They're a-goin' to lock him up, and I'll never see him no more."

"Oh, yes, you will," said the officer, good-naturedly; "he's there in that first patrol-wagon. You can run over and say good night to him, and then you'd better get to bed. This ain't no place for kids of your age."

"Thank you, sir," sniffed Gallegher, tearfully, as the two officers raised their clubs, and let him pass out into the darkness.

The yard outside was in a tumult, horses were stamping, and plunging, and backing the carriages into one another; lights were flashing from every window of what had been apparently an uninhabited house, and the voices of the prisoners were still raised in angry expostulation.

Three police patrol-wagons were moving about the yard, filled with unwilling passengers, who sat or stood, packed together like sheep, and with no protection from the sleet and rain.

Gallegher stole off into a dark corner, and watched the scene until his eyesight became familiar with the position of the land.

Then with his eyes fixed fearfully on the swinging light of a lantern with which an officer was searching among the carriages, he groped his way between horses' hoofs and behind the wheels of carriages to the cab which he had himself placed at the furthermost gate. It was still there, and the horse, as he had left it, with its head turned toward the city. Gallegher opened the big gate noiselessly, and worked nervously at the hitching strap. The knot was covered with a thin coating of ice, and it was several minutes before he could loosen it. But his teeth finally pulled it apart, and with the reins in his hands he sprang upon the wheel. ·And as he stood so, a shock of fear ran down his back like an electric current, his breath left him, and he stood immovable, gazing with wide eyes into the darkness.

The officer with the lantern had suddenly loomed up from behind a carriage not fifty feet distant, and was standing perfectly still, with his lantern held over his head, peering so directly toward Gallegher that the boy felt that he must see him. Gallegher stood with one foot on the hub of the wheel and with the other on the box waiting to spring. It seemed a minute before either of them moved, and then the officer took a step forward, and demanded sternly, "Who is that? What are you doing there?"

There was no time for parley then. Gallegher felt that he had been taken in the act, and that his only chance lay in open flight. He leaped up on the box, pulling out the whip as he did so, and with a quick sweep lashed the horse across the head and back. The animal sprang forward with a snort, narrowly clearing the gate-post, and plunged off into the darkness.

"Stop!" cried the officer.

So many of Gallegher's acquaintances among the 'longshoremen and mill hands had been challenged in so much the same manner that Gallegher knew what would probably follow if the challenge was disregarded. So he slipped from his seat to the footboard below, and ducked his head.

The three reports of a pistol, which rang out briskly from behind him, proved that his early training had given him a valuable fund of useful miscellaneous knowledge.

"Don't you be scared," he said, reassuringly, to the horse; "he's firing in the air."

The pistol-shots were answered by the impatient clangor of a patrol-wagon's gong, and glancing over his shoulder Gallegher saw its red and green lanterns tossing from side to side and looking in the darkness like the side-lights of a yacht plunging forward in a storm.

"I hadn't bargained to race you against no patrol-wagons," said Gallegher to his animal; "but if they want a race, we'll give them a tough tussle for it, won't we?"

Philadelphia, lying four miles to the south, sent up a faint yellow glow to the sky. It seemed very far away, and Gallegher's braggadocio grew cold within him at the loneliness of his adventure and the thought of the long ride before him.

It was still bitterly cold.

The rain and sleet beat through his clothes, and struck his skin with a sharp chilling touch that set him trembling.

Even the thought of the over-weighted patrol-wagon probably sticking in the mud some safe distance in the rear, failed to cheer him, and the excitement that had so far made him callous to the cold died out and left him weaker and nervous. But his horse was chilled with the long standing, and now leaped eagerly forward, only too willing to warm the half-frozen blood in its veins.

"You're a good beast," said Gallegher, plaintively. "You've got more nerve than me. Don't you go back on me now. Mr. Dwyer says we've got to beat the town." Gallegher had no idea what time it was as he rode through the night, but he knew he would be able to find out from a big clock over a manufactory at a point nearly three-quarters of the distance from Keppler's to the goal.

He was still in the open country and driving recklessly, for he knew the best part of his ride must be made outside the city limits.

He raced between desolate-looking corn-fields with bare stalks and patches of muddy earth rising above the thin covering of snow, truck farms and brick-yards fell behind him on either side. It was very lonely work, and once or twice the dogs ran yelping to the gates and barked after him.

Part of his way lay parallel with the railroad tracks, and he drove for some time beside long lines of freight and coal cars as they stood resting for the night. The fantastic Queen Anne suburban stations were dark and deserted, but in one or two of the block-towers he could see the operators writing at their desks, and the sight in some way comforted him.

Once he thought of stopping to get out the blanket in which he had wrapped himself on the first trip, but he feared to spare the time, and drove on with his teeth chattering and his shoulders shaking with the cold.

He welcomed the first solitary row of darkened houses with a faint cheer of recognition. The scattered lamp-posts lightened his spirits, and even the badly paved streets rang under the beats of his horse's feet like music. Great mills and manufactories, with only a night-watchman's light in the lowest of their many stories, began to take the place of the gloomy farm-houses and gaunt trees that had startled him with their grotesque shapes. He had been driving nearly an hour, he calculated, and in that time the rain had changed to a wet snow, that fell heavily and clung to whatever it touched. He passed block after block of trim workmen's houses, as still and silent as the sleepers within them, and at last he turned the horse's head into Broad Street, the city's great thoroughfare, that stretches from its one end to the other and cuts it evenly in two.

He was driving noiselessly over the snow and slush in the street, with his thoughts bent only on the clock-face he wished so much to see, when a hoarse voice challenged him from the sidewalk. "Hey, you, stop there, hold up!" said the voice.

Gallegher turned his head, and though he saw that the voice came from under a policeman's helmet, his only answer was to hit his horse sharply over the head with his whip and to urge it into a gallop.

This, on his part, was followed by a sharp, shrill whistle from the policeman. Another whistle answered it from a street-corner one block ahead of him. "Whoa," said Gallegher, pulling on the reins. "There's one too many of them," he added, in apologetic explanation. The horse stopped, and stood, breathing heavily, with great clouds of steam rising from its flanks.

"Why in hell didn't you stop when I told you to?" demanded the voice, now close at the cab's side.

"I didn't hear you," returned Gallegher, sweetly. "But I heard you whistle, and I heard your partner whistle, and I thought maybe it was me you wanted to speak to, so I just stopped."

"You heard me well enough. Why aren't your lights lit?" demanded the voice.

"Should I have 'em lit?" asked Gallegher, bending over and regarding them with sudden interest.

"You know you should, and if you don't, you've no right to be driving that cab. I don't believe you're the regular driver, anyway. Where'd you get it?"

"It ain't my cab, of course," said Gallegher, with an easy laugh. "It's Luke McGovern's. He left it outside Cronin's while he went in to get a drink, and he took too much, and me father told me to drive it round to the stable for him. I'm Cronin's son. McGovern ain't in no condition to drive. You can see yourself how he's been misusing the horse. He puts it up at Bachman's livery stable, and I was just going around there now."

Gallegher's knowledge of the local celebrities of the district confused the zealous officer of the peace. He surveyed the boy with a steady stare that would have distressed a less skilful liar, but Gallegher only shrugged his shoulders slightly, as if from the cold, and waited with apparent indifference to what the officer would say next.

In reality his heart was beating heavily against his side, and he felt that if he was kept on a strain much longer he would give way and break down. A second snow-covered form emerged suddenly from the shadow of the houses.

"What is it, Reeder?" it asked.

"Oh, nothing much," replied the first officer.

"This kid hadn't any lamps lit, so I called to him to stop and he didn't do it, so I whistled to you. It's all right, though. He's just taking it round to Bachman's. Go ahead," he added, sulkily.

"Get up!" chirped Gallegher. "Good night," he added, over his shoulder.

Gallegher gave an hysterical little gasp of relief as he trotted away from the two policemen, and poured bitter maledictions on their heads for two meddling fools as he went.

"They might as well kill a man as scare him to death," he said, with an attempt to get back to his customary flippancy. But the effort was somewhat pitiful, and he felt guiltily conscious that a salt, warm tear was creeping slowly down his face, and that a lump that would not keep down was rising in his throat.

"'Tain't no fair thing for the whole police force to keep worrying at a little boy like me," he said, in shame-faced apology. "I'm not doing nothing wrong, and I'm half froze to death, and yet they keep a-nagging at me."

It was so cold that when the boy stamped his feet against the footboard to keep them warm, sharp pains shot up through his body, and when he beat his arms about his shoulders, as he had seen real cabmen do, the blood in his finger-tips tingled so acutely that he cried aloud with the pain.

He had often been up that late before, but he had never felt so sleepy. It was as if some one was pressing a sponge heavy with chloroform near his face, and he could not fight off the drowsiness that lay hold of him.

He saw, dimly hanging above his head, a round disc of light that seemed like a great moon, and which he finally guessed to be the clock-face for which he had been on the look-out. He had passed it before he realized this; but the fact stirred him into wakefulness again, and when his cab's wheels slipped around the City Hall corner, he remembered to look up at the other big clock-face that keeps awake over the railroad station and measures out the night.

He gave a gasp of consternation when he saw that it was half-past two, and that there was but ten minutes left to him. This, and the many electric lights and the sight of the familiar pile of buildings, startled him into

Richard Harding Davis

a semi-consciousness of where he was and how great was the necessity for haste.

He rose in his seat and called on the horse, and urged it into a reckless gallop over the slippery asphalt. He considered nothing else but speed, and looking neither to the left nor right dashed off down Broad Street into Chestnut, where his course lay straight away to the office, now only seven blocks distant.

Gallegher never knew how it began, but he was suddenly assaulted by shouts on either side, his horse was thrown back on its haunches, and he found two men in cabmen's livery hanging at its head, and patting its sides, and calling it by name. And the other cabmen who have their stand at the corner were swarming about the carriage, all of them talking and swearing at once, and gesticulating wildly with their whips.

They said they knew the cab was McGovern's, and they wanted to know where he was, and why he wasn't on it; they wanted to know where Gallegher had stolen it, and why he had been such a fool as to drive it into the arms of its owner's friends; they said that it was about time that a cab-driver could get off his box to take a drink without having his cab run away with, and some of them called loudly for a policeman to take the young thief in charge.

Gallegher felt as if he had been suddenly dragged into consciousness out of a bad dream, and stood for a second like a half-awakened somnambulist.

They had stopped the cab under an electric light, and its glare shone coldly down upon the trampled snow and the faces of the men around him.

Gallegher bent forward, and lashed savagely at the horse with his whip.

"Let me go," he shouted, as he tugged impotently at the reins. "Let me go, I tell you. I haven't stole no cab, and you've got no right to stop me. I only want to take it to the *Press* office," he begged. "They'll send it back to you all right. They'll pay you for the trip. I'm not running away with it. The driver's got the collar - he's 'rested - and I'm only a-going to the *Press* office. Do you hear me?" he cried, his voice rising and breaking in a shriek of passion and disappointment. "I tell you to let go those reins. Let me go, or I'll kill you. Do you hear me? I'll kill you." And leaning forward, the boy struck savagely with his long whip at the faces of the men about the horse's head.

Some one in the crowd reached up and caught him by the ankles, and with a quick jerk pulled him off the box, and threw him on to the street. But he was up on his knees in a moment, and caught at the man's hand.

"Don't let them stop me, mister," he cried, "please let me go. I didn't steal the cab, sir. S'help me, I didn't. I'm telling you the truth. Take me to the *Press* office, and they'll prove it to you. They'll pay you anything you ask 'em. It's only such a little ways now, and I've come so far, sir. Please don't let them stop me," he sobbed, clasping the man about the knees. "For Heaven's sake, mister, let me go!"

The managing editor of the *Press* took up the india-rubber speaking- tube at his side, and answered, "Not yet" to an inquiry the night editor had already put to him five times within the last twenty minutes.

Richard Harding Davis

Then he snapped the metal top of the tube impatiently, and went up-stairs. As he passed the door of the local room, he noticed that the reporters had not gone home, but were sitting about on the tables and chairs, waiting. They looked up inquiringly as he passed, and the city editor asked, "Any news yet?" and the managing editor shook his head.

The compositors were standing idle in the composing-room, and their foreman was talking with the night editor.

"Well," said that gentleman, tentatively.

"Well," returned the managing editor, "I don't think we can wait; do you?"

"It's a half-hour after time now," said the night editor, "and we'll miss the suburban trains if we hold the paper back any longer. We can't afford to wait for a purely hypothetical story. The chances are all against the fight's having taken place or this Hade's having been arrested."

"But if we're beaten on it - " suggested the chief. "But I don't think that is possible. If there were any story to print, Dwyer would have had it here before now."

The managing editor looked steadily down at the floor.

"Very well," he said, slowly, "we won't wait any longer. Go ahead," he added, turning to the foreman with a sigh of reluctance. The foreman whirled himself about, and began to give his orders; but the two editors still looked at each other doubtfully.

As they stood so, there came a sudden shout and the sound of people running to and fro in the reportorial rooms below. There was the tramp of many footsteps on the stairs, and above the confusion they heard the voice of the city editor telling some one to "run to Madden's and get some brandy, quick."

No one in the composing-room said anything; but those compositors who had started to go home began slipping off their overcoats, and every one stood with his eyes fixed on the door.

It was kicked open from the outside, and in the doorway stood a cab-driver and the city editor, supporting between them a pitiful little figure of a boy, wet and miserable, and with the snow melting on his clothes and running in little pools to the floor. "Why, it's Gallegher," said the night editor, in a tone of the keenest disappointment.

Gallegher shook himself free from his supporters, and took an unsteady step forward, his fingers fumbling stiffly with the buttons of his waistcoat.

"Mr. Dwyer, sir," he began faintly, with his eyes fixed fearfully on the managing editor, "he got arrested - and I couldn't get here no sooner, 'cause they kept a-stopping me, and they took me cab from under me - but -" he pulled the notebook from his breast and held it out with its covers damp and limp from the rain, "but we got Hade, and here's Mr. Dwyer's copy."

And then he asked, with a queer note in his voice, partly of dread and partly of hope, "Am I in time, sir?"

The managing editor took the book, and tossed it to the

foreman, who ripped out its leaves and dealt them out to his men as rapidly as a gambler deals out cards.

Then the managing editor stooped and picked Gallegher up in his arms, and, sitting down, began to unlace his wet and muddy shoes.

Gallegher made a faint effort to resist this degradation of the managerial dignity; but his protest was a very feeble one, and his head fell back heavily on the managing editor's shoulder.

To Gallegher the incandescent lights began to whirl about in circles, and to burn in different colors; the faces of the reporters kneeling before him and chafing his hands and feet grew dim and unfamiliar, and the roar and rumble of the great presses in the basement sounded far away, like the murmur of the sea.

And then the place and the circumstances of it came back to him again sharply and with sudden vividness.

Gallegher looked up, with a faint smile, into the managing editor's face. "You won't turn me off for running away, will you?" he whispered.

The managing editor did not answer immediately. His head was bent, and he was thinking, for some reason or other, of a little boy of his own, at home in bed. Then he said, quietly, "Not this time, Gallegher."

Gallegher's head sank back comfortably on the older man's shoulder, and he smiled comprehensively at the faces of the young men crowded around him. "You hadn't ought to," he said, with a touch of his old impudence, "'cause - I beat the town."

A WALK UP THE AVENUE

He came down the steps slowly, and pulling mechanically at his gloves.

He remembered afterwards that some woman's face had nodded brightly to him from a passing brougham, and that he had lifted his hat through force of habit, and without knowing who she was.

He stopped at the bottom of the steps, and stood for a moment uncertainly, and then turned toward the north, not because he had any definite goal in his mind, but because the other way led toward his rooms, and he did not want to go there yet.

He was conscious of a strange feeling of elation, which he attributed to his being free, and to the fact that he was his own master again in everything. And with this he confessed to a distinct feeling of littleness, of having acted meanly or unworthily of himself or of her.

And yet he had behaved well, even quixotically. He had tried to leave the impression with her that it was her wish, and that she had broken with him, not he with her.

He held a man who threw a girl over as something

Richard Harding Davis

contemptible, and he certainly did not want to appear to himself in that light; or, for her sake, that people should think he had tired of her, or found her wanting in any one particular. He knew only too well how people would talk. How they would say he had never really cared for her; that he didn't know his own mind when he had proposed to her; and that it was a great deal better for her as it is than if he had grown out of humor with her later. As to their saying she had jilted him, he didn't mind that. He much preferred they should take that view of it, and he was chivalrous enough to hope she would think so too.

He was walking slowly, and had reached Thirtieth Street. A great many young girls and women had bowed to him or nodded from the passing carriages, but it did not tend to disturb the measure of his thoughts. He was used to having people put themselves out to speak to him; everybody made a point of knowing him, not because he was so very handsome and well-looking, and an over-popular youth, but because he was as yet unspoiled by it.

But, in any event, he concluded, it was a miserable business. Still, he had only done what was right. He had seen it coming on for a month now, and how much better it was that they should separate now than later, or that they should have had to live separated in all but location for the rest of their lives! Yes, he had done the right thing - decidedly the only thing to do.

He was still walking up the Avenue, and had reached Thirty-second Street, at which point his thoughts received a sudden turn. A half-dozen men in a club window nodded to him, and brought to him sharply what he was going back to. He had dropped out of their lives as entirely of late as though he had been living in a distant city. When he had met them he had found their company uninteresting and unprofitable. He had wondered how he had ever cared for that sort of thing, and where had been the pleasure of it. Was he going back now to the gossip of that window, to the heavy discussions of traps and horses, to late breakfasts and early suppers? Must he listen to their congratulations on his being one of them again, and must he guess at their whispered conjectures as to how soon it would be before he again took up the chains and harness of their fashion? He struck the pavement sharply with his stick. No, he was not going back.

She had taught him to find amusement and occupation in many things that were better and higher than any pleasures or pursuits he had known before, and he could not give them up. He had her to thank for that at least. And he would give her credit for it too, and gratefully. He would always remember it, and he would show in his way of living the influence and the good effects of these three months in which they had been continually together.

He had reached Forty-second Street now. Well, it was over with, and he would get to work at something or other. This experience had shown him that he was not meant for marriage; that he was intended to live alone. Because, if he found that a girl as lovely as she undeniably was palled on him after three months, it was evident that he would never live through life with any other one. Yes, he would always be a bachelor. He had lived his life, had told his story at the age of twenty-five, and would wait patiently for the end, a marked and gloomy man. He would travel now and see the world. He would go to that hotel in Cairo she was always talking about, where they were to have gone on their honeymoon; or he might strike further into Africa, and come back bronzed and worn with long marches and jungle fever, and with his hair prematurely white. He even considered himself, with great self-pity, returning and finding her married and happy, of course. And he enjoyed, in anticipation, the secret doubts she would have of her later choice when she heard on all sides praise of this distinguished traveller.

And he pictured himself meeting her reproachful glances with fatherly friendliness, and presenting her husband with tiger-skins, and buying her children extravagant presents.

This was at Forty-fifth Street.

Yes, that was decidedly the best thing to do. To go away and improve himself, and study up all those painters and cathedrals with which she was so hopelessly conversant.

He remembered how out of it she had once made him feel, and how secretly he had admired her when she had referred to a modern painting as looking like those in the long gallery of the Louvre. He thought he knew all about the Louvre, but he would go over again and locate that long gallery, and become able to talk to her understandingly about it.

And then it came over him like a blast of icy air that he could never talk over things with her again. He had reached Fifty-fifth Street now, and the shock brought him to a standstill on the corner, where he stood gazing blankly before him. He felt rather weak physically, and decided to go back to his rooms, and then he pictured how cheerless they would look, and how little of comfort they contained. He had used them only to dress and sleep in of late, and the distaste with which he regarded the idea that he must go back to them to read and sit and live in them, showed him how utterly his life had become bound up with the house on Twenty-seventh Street.

"Where was he to go in the evening?" he asked himself, with pathetic hopelessness, "or in the morning or afternoon for that matter?" Were there to be no more of those journeys to picture-galleries and to the big publishing houses, where they used to hover over the new book counter and pull the books about, and make each other innumerable presents of daintily bound volumes, until the clerks grew to know them so well that they never went through the form of asking where the books were to be sent? And those tete-a-tete luncheons at her house when her mother was upstairs with a headache or a dressmaker, and the long rides and walks in the Park in the afternoon, and the rush down town to dress, only to return to dine with them, ten minutes late always, and always with some new excuse, which was allowed if it was clever, and frowned at if it was common-place - was all this really over?

Why, the town had only run on because she was in it, and as he walked the streets the very shop windows had suggested her to him - florists only existed that he might send her flowers, and gowns and bonnets in the milliners' windows were only pretty as they would become her; and as for the theatres and the news-papers, they were only worth while as they gave her pleasure. And he had given all this up, and for what, he asked himself, and why?

He could not answer that now. It was simply because he had been surfeited with too much content, he replied, passionately. He had not appreciated how happy he had been. She had been too kind, too gracious. He had never known until he had quarrelled with her and lost her how precious and dear she had been to him.

He was at the entrance to the Park now, and he strode on along the walk, bitterly upbraiding himself for being worse than a criminal - a fool, a common blind mortal to whom a goddess had stooped.

He remembered with bitter regret a turn off the drive into which they had wandered one day, a secluded, pretty spot with a circle of box around it, and into the turf of which he had driven his stick, and claimed it for them both by the right of discovery. And he recalled how they had used to go there, just out of sight of their friends in the ride, and sit and chatter on a green bench beneath a bush of box, like any nursery maid and her young man, while her groom stood at the brougham door in the bridle-path beyond. He had broken off a sprig of the box one day and given it to her, and she had kissed it foolishly, and laughed, and hidden it in the folds of her riding-skirt, in burlesque fear lest the guards should arrest them for breaking the much-advertised ordinance.

And he remembered with a miserable smile how she had delighted him with her account of her adventure to her mother, and described them as fleeing down the Avenue with their treasure, pursued by a squadron of mounted policemen.

This and a hundred other of the foolish, happy fancies they had shared in common came back to him, and he remembered how she had stopped one cold afternoon just outside of this favorite spot, beside an open iron grating sunk in the path, into which the rain had washed the autumn leaves, and pretended it was a steam radiator, and held her slim gloved hands out over it as if to warm them.

How absurdly happy she used to make him, and how light-hearted she had been! He determined suddenly and sentimentally to go to that secret place now, and bury the engagement ring she had handed back to him under that bush as he had buried his hopes of happiness, and he pictured how some day when he was dead she would read of this in his will, and go and dig up the ring, and remember and forgive him. He struck off from the walk across the turf straight toward this dell, taking the ring from his waistcoat pocket and clinching it in his hand. He was walking quickly with rapt interest in this idea of abnegation when he noticed, unconsciously at first and then with a start, the familiar outlines and colors of her brougham drawn up in the drive not twenty yards from their old meeting-place. He could not be mistaken; he knew the horses well enough, and there was old Wallis on the box and young Wallis on the path.

He stopped breathlessly, and then tipped on cautiously, keeping the encircling line of bushes between him and the carriage. And then he saw through the leaves that there was some one in the place, and that it was she. He stopped, confused and amazed. He could not comprehend it. She must have driven to the place immediately on his departure. But why? And why to that place of all others?

He parted the bushes with his hands, and saw her lovely and sweet-looking as she had always been, standing under the box bush beside the bench, and breaking off one of the green branches. The branch parted and the stem flew back to its place again, leaving a green sprig in her hand. She turned at that moment directly toward him, and he could see from his hiding-place how she lifted the leaves to her lips, and that a tear was creeping down her cheek.

Then he dashed the bushes aside with both arms, and with a cry that no one but she heard sprang toward her.

Young Van Bibber stopped his mail phaeton in front of the club, and went inside to recuperate, and told how he had seen them driving home through the Park in her brougham and unchaperoned.

"Which I call very bad form," said the punctilious Van Bibber, "even though they are engaged."

MY DISREPUTABLE FRIEND, MR. RAEGEN

Rags Raegen was out of his element. The water was his proper element - the water of the East River by preference. And when it came to "running the roofs," as he would have himself expressed it, he was "not in it."

On those other occasions when he had been followed by the police, he had raced them toward the river front and had dived boldly in from the wharf, leaving them staring blankly and in some alarm as to his safety. Indeed, three different men in the precinct, who did not know of young Raegen's aquatic prowess, had returned to the station-house and seriously reported him to the sergeant as lost, and regretted having driven a citizen into the river, where he had been unfortunately drowned. It was even told how, on one occasion, when hotly followed, young Raegen had dived off Wakeman's Slip, at East Thirty-third Street, and had then swum back under water to the landing-steps, while the policeman and a crowd of stevedores stood watching for him to reappear where he had sunk. It is further related that he had then, in a spirit of recklessness, and in the possibility of the policeman's failing to recognize him, pushed his way through the crowd from the rear and plunged in to rescue the supposedly drowned man. And that after two or three futile attempts to find his own corpse, he had climbed up on the dock and told the officer that he had touched the body sticking in the mud. And, as a result of this fiction, the river-police dragged the river-bed around Wakeman's Slip with grappling irons for four hours, while Rags sat on the wharf and directed their movements.

But on this present occasion the police were standing between him and the river, and so cut off his escape in that direction, and as they had seen him strike McGonegal and had seen McGonegal fall, he had to run for it and seek refuge on the roofs. What made it worse was that he was not in his own hunting-grounds, but in McGonegal's, and while any tenement on Cherry Street would have given him shelter, either for love of him or fear of him, these of Thirty-third Street were against him and "all that Cherry Street gang," while "Pike" McGonegal was their darling and their hero. And, if Rags had known it, any tenement on the block was better than Case's, into which he first turned, for Case's was empty and untenanted, save in one or two rooms, and the opportunities for dodging from one to another were in consequence very few. But he could not know this, and so he plunged into the dark hall-way and sprang up the first four flights of stairs, three steps at a jump, with one arm stretched out in front of him, for it was very dark and the turns were short. On the fourth floor he fell headlong over a bucket with a broom sticking in it, and cursed whoever left it there. There was a ladder leading from the sixth floor to the roof, and he ran up this and drew it after him as he fell forward out of the wooden trap that opened on the flat tin roof like a companion-way of a ship. The chimneys would have hidden him, but there was a policeman's helmet coming up from another companion-way, and he saw that the Italians hanging out of the windows of the other tenements were pointing at him and showing him to the officer. So he hung by his hands and dropped back again. It was not much of a fall, but it jarred him, and the race he had already run had nearly taken his breath from him. For Rags did not live a life calculated to fit young men for sudden trials of speed.

He stumbled back down the narrow stairs, and, with a vivid recollection of the bucket he had already fallen upon, felt his way cautiously with his hands and with one foot stuck out in front of him. If he had been in his own bailiwick, he would have rather enjoyed the tense excitement of the chase than otherwise, for there he was at home and knew all the cross-cuts and where to find each broken paling in the roof-fences, and all the traps in the roofs. But here he was running in a maze, and what looked like a safe passage-way might throw him head on into the outstretched arms of the officers.

And while he felt his way his mind was terribly acute to the fact that as yet no door on any of the landings had been thrown open to him, either curiously or hospitably as offering a place of refuge. He did not want to be taken, but in spite of this he was quite cool, and so, when he heard quick, heavy footsteps beating up the stairs, he stopped himself suddenly by placing one hand on the side of the wall and the other on the banister and halted, panting. He could distinguish from below the high voices of women and children and excited men in the street, and as the steps came nearer he heard some one lowering the ladder he had thrown upon the roof to the sixth floor and preparing to descend. "Ah!" snarled Raegen, panting and desperate, "youse think you have me now, sure, don't you?" It rather frightened him to find the house so silent, for, save the footsteps of the officers, descending and ascending upon him, he seemed to be the only living person in all the dark, silent building.

He did not want to fight.

He was under heavy bonds already to keep the peace, and this last had surely been in self-defence, and he felt he could prove it. What he wanted now was to get away, to get back to his own people and to lie hidden in his own cellar or garret, where they would feed and guard him until the trouble was over. And still, like the two ends of a vise, the representatives of the law were closing in upon him. He turned the knob of the door opening to the landing on which he stood, and tried to push it in, but it was locked. Then he stepped quickly to the door on the opposite side and threw his shoulder against it. The door opened, and he stumbled forward sprawling. The room in which he had taken refuge was almost bare, and very dark; but in a little room leading from it he saw a pile of tossed-up bedding on the floor, and he dived at this as though it was water, and crawled far under it until he reached the wall beyond, squirming on his face and stomach, and flattening out his arms and legs. Then he lay motionless, holding back his breath, and listening to the beating of his heart and to the footsteps on the stairs. The footsteps stopped on the landing leading to the outer room, and he could hear the murmur of voices as the two men questioned one another. Then the door was kicked open, and there was a long silence, broken sharply by the click of a revolver.

"Maybe he's in there," said a bass voice. The men stamped across the floor leading into the dark room in which he lay, and halted at the entrance. They did not stand there over a moment before they turned and moved away again; but to Raegen, lying with blood-vessels choked, and with his hand pressed across his mouth, it seemed as if they had been contemplating and enjoying his agony for over an hour. "I was in this place not more than twelve hours ago," said one of them easily. "I come in to take a couple out for fighting. They were yelling 'murder' and 'police,' and breaking things; but they went quiet enough. The man is a stevedore, I guess, and him and his wife used to get drunk regular and carry on up here every night or so. They got thirty days on the Island."

"Who's taking care of the rooms?" asked the bass voice. The first voice said he guessed "no one was," and added: "There ain't much to take care of, that I can see." "That's so," assented the bass voice. "Well," he went on briskly, "he's not here; but he's in the building, sure, for he put back when he seen me coming over the roof. And he didn't pass me, neither, I know that, anyway," protested the bass voice. Then the bass voice said that he must have slipped into the flat below, and added something that Raegen could not hear distinctly, about Schaffer on the roof, and their having him safe enough, as that red-headed cop from the Eighteenth Precinct was watching on the street. They closed the door behind them, and their footsteps clattered down the stairs, leaving the big house silent and apparently deserted. Young Raegen raised his head, and let his breath escape with a great gasp of relief, as when he had been a long time under water, and cautiously rubbed the perspiration out of his eyes and from his forehead. It had been a cruelly hot, close afternoon, and the stifling burial under the heavy bedding, and the excitement, had left him feverishly hot and trembling. It was already growing dark outside, although he could not know that until he lifted the quilts an inch or two and peered up at the dirty window-panes. He was afraid to rise, as yet, and flattened himself out with an impatient sigh, as he gathered the bedding over his head again and held back his breath to listen. There may have been a minute or more of absolute silence in which he lay there, and then his blood froze to ice in his veins, his breath stopped, and he heard, with a quick gasp of terror, the sound of something crawling toward him across the floor of the outer room. The instinct of self-defence moved him first to leap to his feet, and to face and fight it, and then followed as quickly a foolish sense of safety in his hiding-place; and he called upon his greatest strength, and, by his mere brute will alone, forced his forehead down to the bare floor and lay rigid, though his nerves jerked with unknown, unreasoning fear. And still he heard the sound of this living thing coming creeping toward him until the instinctive terror that shook him overcame his will, and he threw the bed-clothes from him with a hoarse cry, and sprang up trembling to his feet, with his back against the wall, and with his arms thrown out in front of him wildly, and with the willingness in them and the power in them to do murder.

The room was very dark, but the windows of the one beyond let in a little stream of light across the floor, and in this light he saw moving toward him on its hands and knees a little baby who smiled and nodded at him with a pleased look of recognition and kindly welcome.

The fear upon Raegen had been so strong and the reaction was so great that he dropped to a sitting posture on the heap of bedding and laughed long and weakly, and still with a feeling in his heart that this apparition was something strangely unreal and menacing.

But the baby seemed well pleased with his laughter, and stopped to throw back its head and smile and coo and laugh gently with him as though the joke was a very good one which they shared in common. Then it struggled solemnly to its feet and came pattering toward him on a run, with both bare arms held out, and with a look of such confidence in him, and welcome in its face, that Raegen stretched out his arms and closed the baby's fingers fearfully and gently in his own.

He had never seen so beautiful a child. There was dirt enough on its hands and face, and its torn dress was soiled with streaks of coal and ashes. The dust of the floor had rubbed into its bare knees, but the face was like no other face that Rags had ever seen. And then it looked at him as though it trusted him, and just as though they had known each other at some time long before, but the eyes of the baby somehow seemed to hurt him so that he had to turn his face away, and when he looked again it was with a strangely new feeling of dissatisfaction with himself and of wishing to ask pardon. They were wonderful eyes, black and rich, and with a deep superiority of knowledge in them, a knowledge that seemed to be above the knowledge of evil; and when the baby smiled at him, the eyes smiled too with confidence and tenderness in them that in some way frightened Rags and made him move uncomfortably. "Did you know that youse scared me so that I was going to kill you?" whispered Rags, apologetically, as he carefully held the baby from him at arm's length. "Did you?" But the baby only smiled at this and reached out its hand and stroked Rag's cheek with its fingers. There was something so wonderfully soft and sweet in this that Rags drew the baby nearer and gave a quick, strange gasp of pleasure as it threw its arms around his neck and brought the face up close to his chin and hugged him tightly. The baby's arms were very soft and plump, and its cheek and tangled hair were warm and moist with perspiration, and the breath that fell on Raegen's face was sweeter than anything he had ever known. He felt wonderfully and for some reason uncomfortably happy, but the silence was oppressive.

"What's your name, little 'un?" said Rags. The baby ran its arms more closely around Raegen's neck and did not speak, unless its cooing in Raegen's ear was an answer. "What did you say your name was?" persisted Raegen, in a whisper. The baby frowned at this and stopped cooing long enough to say: "Marg'ret," mechanically and without apparently associating the name with herself or anything else. "Margaret, eh!" said Raegen, with grave consideration. "It's a very pretty name," he added, politely, for he could not shake off the feeling that he was in the presence of a superior being. "An' what did you say your dad's name was?" asked Raegen, awkwardly. But this was beyond the baby's patience or knowledge, and she waived the question aside with both arms and began to beat a tattoo gently with her two closed fists on Raegen's chin and throat. "You're mighty strong now, ain't you?" mocked the young giant, laughing. "Perhaps you don't know, Missie," he added, gravely, "that your dad and mar are doing time on the Island, and you won't see 'em again for a month." No, the baby did not know this nor care apparently; she seemed content with Rags and with his company. Sometimes she drew away and looked at him long and dubiously, and this cut Rags to the heart, and he felt guilty, and unreasonably anxious until she smiled reassuringly again and ran back into his arms, nestling her face against his and stroking his rough chin wonderingly with her little fingers.

Rags forgot the lateness of the night and the darkness that fell upon the room in the interest of this strange entertainment, which was so much more absorbing, and so much more innocent than any other he had ever known. He almost forgot the fact that he lay in hiding, that he was surrounded by unfriendly neighbors, and that at any moment the representatives of local justice might come in and rudely lead him away. For this reason he dared not make a light, but he moved his position so that the glare from an electric lamp on the street outside might fall across the baby's face, as it lay alternately dozing and awakening, to smile up at him in the bend of his arm. Once it reached inside the collar of his shirt and pulled out the scapular that hung around his neck, and looked at it so long, and with such apparent seriousness, that Rags was confirmed in his fear that this kindly visitor was something more or less of a superhuman agent, and his efforts to make this supposition coincide with the fact that the angel's parents were on Blackwell's Island, proved one of the severest struggles his mind had ever experienced. He had forgotten to feel hungry, and the knowledge that he was acutely so, first came to him with the thought that the baby must obviously be in greatest need of food herself. This pained him greatly, and he laid his burden down upon the bedding, and after slipping off his shoes, tip-toed his way across the room on a foraging expedition after something she could eat. There was a half of a ham-bone, and a half loaf of hard bread in a cupboard, and on the table he found a bottle quite filled with wretched whiskey. That the police had failed to see the baby had not appealed to him in any way, but that they should have allowed this last find to remain unnoticed pleased him intensely, not because it now fell to him, but because they had been cheated of it. It really struck him as so humorous that he stood laughing silently for several minutes, slapping his thigh with every outward exhibition of the keenest mirth. But when he found that the room and cupboard were bare of anything else that might be eaten he sobered suddenly. It was very hot, and though the windows were open, the perspiration stood upon his face, and the foul close air that rose from the court and street below made him gasp and pant for breath. He dipped a wash rag in the water from the spigot in the hall, and filled a cup with it and bathed the baby's face and wrists. She woke and sipped up the water from the cup eagerly, and then looked up at him, as if to ask for something more. Rags soaked the crusty bread in the water, and put it to the baby's lips, but after nibbling at it eagerly she shook her head and looked up at him again with such reproachful pleading in her eyes, that Rags felt her silence more keenly than the worst abuse he had ever received.

It hurt him so, that the pain brought tears to his eyes.

"Deary girl," he cried, "I'd give you anything you could think of if I had it. But I can't get it, see? It ain't that I don't want to - good Lord, little 'un, you don't think that, do you?"

The baby smiled at this, just as though she understood him, and touched his face as if to comfort him, so that Rags felt that same exquisite content again, which moved him so strangely whenever the child caressed him, and which left him soberly wondering. Then the baby crawled up onto his lap and dropped asleep, while Rags sat motionless and fanned her with a folded newspaper, stopping every now and then to pass the damp cloth over her warm face and arms. It was quite late now. Outside he could hear the neighbors laughing and talking on the roofs, and when one group sang hilariously to an accordion, he cursed them under his breath for noisy, drunken fools, and in his anger lest they should disturb the child in his arms, expressed an anxious hope that they would fall off and break their useless necks. It grew silent and much cooler as the night ran out, but Rags still sat immovable, shivering slightly every now and then and cautiously stretching his stiff legs and body. The arm that held the child grew stiff and numb with the light burden, but he took a fierce pleasure in the pain, and became hardened to it, and at last fell into an uneasy slumber from which he awoke to pass his hands gently over the soft yielding body, and to draw it slowly and closer to him. And then, from very weariness, his eyes closed and his head fell back heavily against the wall, and the man and the child in his arms slept peacefully in the dark corner of the deserted tenement.

The sun rose hissing out of the East River, a broad, red disc of heat. It swept the cross-streets of the city as pitilessly as the search-light of a man-of-war sweeps the ocean. It blazed brazenly into open windows, and changed beds into gridirons on which the sleepers tossed and turned and woke unrefreshed and with throats dry and parched. Its glare awakened Rags into a startled belief that the place about him was on fire, and he stared wildly until the child in his arms brought him back to the knowledge of where he was. He ached in every joint and limb, and his eyes smarted with the dry heat, but the baby concerned him most, for she was breathing with hard, long, irregular gasps, her mouth was open and her absurdly small fists were clenched, and around her closed eyes were deep blue rings. Rags felt a cold rush of fear and uncertainty come over him as he stared about him helplessly for aid. He had seen babies look like this before, in the tenements; they were like this when the young doctors of the Health Board climbed to the roofs to see them, and they were like this, only quiet and still, when the ambulance came clattering up the narrow streets, and bore them away. Rags carried the baby into the outer room, where the sun had not yet penetrated, and laid her down gently on the coverlets; then he let the water in the sink run until it was fairly cool, and with this bathed the baby's face and hands and feet, and lifted a cup of the water to her open lips. She woke at this and smiled again, but very faintly, and when she looked at him he felt fearfully sure that she did not know him, and that she was looking through and past him at something he could not see.

He did not know what to do, and he wanted to do so much. Milk was the only thing he was quite sure babies cared for, but in want of this he made a mess of bits of the dry ham and crumbs of bread, moistened with the raw whiskey, and put it to her lips on the end of a spoon. The baby tasted this, and pushed his hand away, and then looked up and gave a feeble cry, and seemed to say, as plainly as a grown woman could have said or written, "It isn't any use, Rags. You are very good to me, but, indeed, I cannot do it. Don't worry, please; I don't blame you."

"Great Lord," gasped Rags, with a queer choking in his throat, "but ain't she got grit." Then he bethought him of the people who he still believed inhabited the rest of the tenement, and he concluded that as the day was yet so early they might still be asleep, and that while they slept, he could "lift" - as he mentally described the act - whatever they might have laid away for breakfast. Excited with this hope, he ran noiselessly down the stairs in his bare feet, and tried the doors of the different landings. But each he found open and each room bare and deserted. Then it occurred to him that at this hour he might even risk a sally into the street. He had money with him, and the milk-carts and bakers' wagons must be passing every minute. He ran back to get the money out of his coat, delighted with the chance and chiding himself for not having dared to do it sooner. He stood over the baby a moment before he left the room, and flushed like a girl as he stooped and kissed one of the bare arms. "I'm going out to get you some breakfast," he said. "I won't be gone long, but if I should," he added, as he paused and shrugged his shoulders, "I'll send the sergeant after you from the station-house. If I only wasn't under bonds," he muttered, as he slipped down the stairs. "If it wasn't for that they couldn't give me more'n a month at the most, even knowing all they do of me. It was only a street fight, anyway, and there was some there that must have seen him pull his pistol." He stopped at the top of the first flight of stairs and sat down to wait. He could see below the top of the open front door, the pavement and a part of the street beyond, and when he heard the rattle of an approaching cart he ran on down and then, with an oath, turned and broke up-stairs again. He had seen the ward detectives standing together on the opposite side of the street.

"Wot are they doing out a bed at this hour?" he demanded angrily. "Don't they make trouble enough through the day, without prowling around before decent people are up? I wonder, now, if they're after me." He dropped on his knees when he reached the room where the baby lay, and peered cautiously out of the window at the detectives, who had been joined by two other men, with whom they were talking earnestly. Raegen knew the new-comers for two of McGonegal's friends, and concluded, with a momentary flush of pride and self-importance, that the detectives were forced to be up at this early hour solely on his account. But this was followed by the afterthought that he must have hurt McGonegal seriously, and that he was wanted in consequence very much. This disturbed him most, he was surprised to find, because it precluded his going forth in search of food. "I guess I can't get you that milk I was looking for," he said, jocularly, to the baby, for the excitement elated him. "The sun outside isn't good for me health." The baby settled herself in his arms and slept again, which sobered Rags, for he argued it was a bad sign, and his own ravenous appetite warned him how the child suffered. When he again offered her the mixture he had prepared for her, she took it eagerly, and Rags breathed a sigh of satisfaction. Then he ate some of the bread and ham himself and swallowed half the whiskey, and stretched out beside the child and fanned her while she slept. It was something strangely incomprehensible to Rags that he should feel so keen a satisfaction in doing even this little for her, but he gave up wondering, and forgot everything else in watching the strange beauty of the sleeping baby and in the odd feeling of responsibility and self-respect she had brought to him.

He did not feel it coming on, or he would have fought against it, but the heat of the day and the sleeplessness of the night before, and the fumes of the whiskey on his empty stomach, drew him unconsciously into a dull stupor, so that the paper fan slipped from his hand, and he sank back on the bedding into a heavy sleep. When he awoke it was nearly dusk and past six o'clock, as he knew by the newsboys calling the sporting extras on the street below. He sprang up, cursing himself, and filled with bitter remorse.

"I'm a drunken fool, that's what I am," said Rags, savagely. "I've let her lie here all day in the heat with no one to watch her." Margaret was breathing so softly that he could hardly discern any life at all, and his heart almost stopped with fear. He picked her up and fanned and patted her into wakefulness again and then turned desperately to the window and looked down. There was no one he knew or who knew him as far as he could tell on the street, and he determined recklessly to risk another sortie for food.

"Why, it's been near two days that child's gone without eating," he said, with keen self-reproach, "and here you've let her suffer to save yourself a trip to the Island. You're a hulking big loafer, you are," he ran on, muttering, "and after her coming to you and taking notice of you and putting her face to yours like an angel." He slipped off his shoes and picked his way cautiously down the stairs.

As he reached the top of the first flight a newsboy passed, calling the evening papers, and shouted something which Rags could not distinguish. He wished he could get a copy of the paper. It might tell him, he thought, something about himself. The boy was coming nearer, and Rags stopped and leaned forward to listen.

"Extry! Extry!" shouted the newsboy, running. "Sun, World, and Mail. Full account of the murder of Pike McGonegal by Ragsey Raegen."

Richard Harding Davis

The lights in the street seemed to flash up suddenly and grow dim again, leaving Rags blind and dizzy.

"Stop," he yelled, "stop. Murdered, no, by God, no," he cried, staggering half-way down the stairs; "stop, stop!" But no one heard Rags, and the sound of his own voice halted him. He sank back weak and sick upon the top step of the stairs and beat his hands together upon his head.

"It's a lie, it's a lie," he whispered, thickly. "I struck him in self-defence, s'help me. I struck him in self-defence. He drove me to it. He pulled his gun on me. I done it in self-defence."

And then the whole appearance of the young tough changed, and the terror and horror that had showed on his face turned to one of low sharpness and evil cunning. His lips drew together tightly and he breathed quickly through his nostrils, while his fingers locked and unlocked around his knees. All that he had learned on the streets and wharves and roof-tops, all that pitiable experience and dangerous knowledge that had made him a leader and a hero among the thieves and bullies of the river-front he called to his assistance now. He faced the fact flatly and with the cool consideration of an uninterested counsellor. He knew that the history of his life was written on Police Court blotters from the day that he was ten years old, and with pitiless detail; that what friends he had he held more by fear than by affection, and that his enemies, who were many, only wanted just such a chance as this to revenge injuries long suffered and bitterly cherished, and that his only safety lay in secret and instant flight. The ferries were watched, of course; he knew that the depots, too, were covered by the men whose only duty was to watch the coming and to halt the departing criminal. But he knew of one old man who was too wise to ask questions and who would row him over the East River to Astoria, and of another on the west side whose boat was always at the disposal of silent white-faced young men who might come at any hour of the night or morning, and whom he would pilot across to the Jersey shore and keep well away from the lights of the passing ferries and the green lamp of the police boat. And once across, he had only to change his name and write for money to be forwarded to that name, and turn to work until the thing was covered up and forgotten. He rose to his feet in his full strength again, and intensely and agreeably excited with the danger, and possibly fatal termination, of his adventure, and then there fell upon him, with the suddenness of a blow, the remembrance of the little child lying on the dirty bedding in the room above.

"I can't do it," he muttered fiercely; "I can't do it," he cried, as if he argued with some other presence. "There's a rope around me neck, and the chances are all against me; it's every man for himself and no favor." He threw his arms out before him as if to push the thought away from him and ran his fingers through his hair and over his face. All of his old self rose in him and mocked him for a weak fool, and showed him just how great his personal danger was, and so he turned and dashed forward on a run, not only to the street, but as if to escape from the other self that held him back. He was still without his shoes, and in his bare feet, and he stopped as he noticed this and turned to go up stairs for them, and then he pictured to himself the baby lying as he had left her, weakly unconscious and with dark rims around her eyes, and he asked himself excitedly what he would do, if, on his return, she should wake and smile and reach out her hands to him.

"I don't dare go back," he said, breathlessly. "I don't dare do it; killing's too good for the likes of Pike McGonegal, but I'm not fighting babies. An' maybe, if I went back, maybe I wouldn't have the nerve to leave her; I can't do it," he muttered, "I don't dare go back." But still he did not stir, but stood motionless, with one hand trembling on the stair-rail and the other clenched beside him, and so fought it on alone in the silence of the empty building.

The lights in the stores below came out one by one, and the minutes passed into half-hours, and still he stood there with the noise of the streets coming up to him below speaking of escape and of a long life of ill-regulated pleasures, and up above him the baby lay in the darkness and reached out her hands to him in her sleep.

The surly old sergeant of the Twenty-first Precinct station-house had read the evening papers through for the third time and was dozing in the fierce lights of the gas-jet over the high desk when a young man with a white, haggard face came in from the street with a baby in his arms.

"I want to see the woman thet look after the station-house - quick," he said.

The surly old sergeant did not like the peremptory tone of the young man nor his general appearance, for he had no hat, nor coat, and his feet were bare; so he said, with deliberate dignity, that the char-woman was up-stairs lying down, and what did the young man want with her? "This child," said the visitor, in a queer thick voice, "she's sick. The heat's come over her, and she ain't had anything to eat for two days, an' she's starving. Ring the bell for the matron, will yer, and send one of your men around for the house surgeon." The sergeant leaned forward comfortably on his elbows, with his hands under his chin so that the gold lace on his cuffs shone effectively in the gaslight. He believed he had a sense of humor and he chose this unfortunate moment to exhibit it.

"Did you take this for a dispensary, young man?" he asked; "or," he continued, with added facetiousness, "a foundling hospital?"

The young man made a savage spring at the barrier in front of the high desk. "Damn you," he panted, "ring that bell, do you hear me, or I'll pull you off that seat and twist your heart out."

The baby cried at this sudden outburst, and Rags fell back, patting it with his hand and muttering between his closed teeth. The sergeant called to the men of the reserve squad in the reading-room beyond, and to humor this desperate visitor, sounded the gong for the janitress. The reserve squad trooped in leisurely with the playing-cards in their hands and with their pipes in their mouths.

"This man," growled the sergeant, pointing with the end of his cigar to Rags, "is either drunk, or crazy, or a bit of both."

The char-woman came down stairs majestically, in a long, loose wrapper, fanning herself with a palm-leaf fan, but when she saw the child, her majesty dropped from her like a cloak, and she ran toward her and caught the baby up in her arms. "You poor little thing," she murmured, "and, oh, how beautiful!" Then she whirled about on the men of the reserve squad: "You, Conners," she said, "run up to my room and get the milk out of my ice-chest; and Moore, put on your coat and go around and tell the surgeon I want to see him. And one of you crack some ice up fine in a towel. Take it out of the cooler. Quick, now."

Raegen came up to her fearfully. "Is she very sick?" he begged; "she ain't going to die, is she?"

"Of course not," said the woman, promptly, "but she's down with the heat, and she hasn't been properly cared for; the child looks half-starved. Are you her father?" she asked, sharply. But Rags did not speak, for at the moment she had answered his question and had said the baby would not die, he had reached out swiftly, and taken the child out of her arms and held it hard against his breast, as though he had lost her and some one had been just giving her back to him.

His head was bending over hers, and so he did not see Wade and Heffner, the two ward detectives, as they came in from the street, looking hot, and tired, and anxious. They gave a careless glance at the group, and then stopped with a start, and one of them gave a long, low whistle.

"Well," exclaimed Wade, with a gasp of surprise and relief. "So Raegen, you're here, after all, are you? Well, you did give us a chase, you did. Who took you?"

The men of the reserve squad, when they heard the name of the man for whom the whole force had been looking for the past two days, shifted their positions slightly, and looked curiously at Rags, and the woman stopped pouring out the milk from the bottle in her hand, and stared at him in frank astonishment. Raegen threw back his head and shoulders, and ran his eyes coldly over the faces of the semicircle of men around him.

"Who took me?" he began defiantly, with a swagger of braggadocio, and then, as though it were hardly worth while, and as though the presence of the baby lifted him above everything else, he stopped, and raised her until her cheek touched his own. It rested there a moment, while Rag stood silent.

"Who took me?" he repeated, quietly, and without lifting his eyes from the baby's face. "Nobody took me," he said. "I gave myself up."

One morning, three months later, when Raegen had stopped his ice-cart in front of my door, I asked him whether at any time he had ever regretted what he had done.

"Well, sir," he said, with easy superiority, "seeing that I've shook the gang, and that the Society's decided her folks ain't fit to take care of her, we can't help thinking we are better off, see?

"But, as for my ever regretting it, why, even when things was at the worst, when the case was going dead against me, and before that cop, you remember, swore to McGonegal's drawing the pistol, and when I used to sit in the Tombs expecting I'd have to hang for it, well, even then, they used to bring her to see me every day, and when they'd lift her up, and she'd reach out her hands and kiss me through the bars, why - they could have took me out and hung me, and been damned to 'em, for all I'd have cared."

THE OTHER WOMAN

Young Latimer stood on one of the lower steps of the hall stairs, leaning with one hand on the broad railing and smiling down at her. She had followed him from the drawing-room and had stopped at the entrance, drawing the curtains behind her, and making, unconsciously, a dark background for her head and figure. He thought he had never seen her look more beautiful, nor that cold, fine air of thorough breeding about her which was her greatest beauty to him, more strongly in evidence.

"Well, sir," she said, "why don't you go?"

He shifted his position slightly and leaned more comfortably upon the railing, as though he intended to discuss it with her at some length.

"How can I go," he said, argumentatively, "with you standing there - looking like that?"

"I really believe," the girl said, slowly, "that he is afraid; yes, he is afraid. And you always said," she added, turning to him, "you were so brave."

"Oh, I am sure I never said that," exclaimed the young man, calmly. "I may be brave, in fact, I am quite brave, but I never said I was. Some one must have told you."

"Yes, he is afraid," she said, nodding her head to the tall clock across the hall, "he is temporizing and trying to save time. And afraid of a man, too, and such a good man who would not hurt any one."

"You know a bishop is always a very difficult sort of a person," he said, "and when he happens to be your father, the combination is just a bit awful. Isn't it now? And especially when one means to ask him for his daughter. You know it isn't like asking him to let one smoke in his study."

"If I loved a girl," she said, shaking her head and smiling up at him, "I wouldn't be afraid of the whole world; that's what they say in books, isn't it? I would be so bold and happy."

"Oh, well, I'm bold enough," said the young man, easily; "if I had not been, I never would have asked you to marry me; and I'm happy enough - that's because I did ask you. But what if he says no," continued the youth; "what if he says he has greater ambitions for you, just as they say in books, too. What will you do? Will you run away with me? I can borrow a coach just as they used to do, and we can drive off through the Park and be married, and come back and ask his blessing on our knees - unless he should overtake us on the elevated."

"That," said the girl, decidedly, "is flippant, and I'm going to leave you. I never thought to marry a man who would be frightened at the very first. I am greatly disappointed."

She stepped back into the drawing-room and pulled the curtains to behind her, and then opened them again and whispered, "Please don't be long," and disappeared. He waited, smiling, to see if she would make another appearance, but she did not, and he heard her touch the keys of the piano at the other end of the drawing-room. And so, still smiling and with her last words sounding in his ears, he walked slowly up the stairs and knocked at the door of the bishop's study. The bishop's room was not ecclesiastic in its character. It looked much like the room of any man of any calling who cared for his books and to have pictures about him, and copies of the beautiful things he had seen on his travels. There were pictures of the Virgin and the Child, but they were those that are seen in almost any house, and there were etchings and plaster casts, and there were hundreds of books, and dark red curtains, and an open fire that lit up the pots of brass with ferns in them, and the blue and white plaques on the top of the bookcase. The bishop sat before his writing-table, with one hand shading his eyes from the light of a red-covered lamp, and looked up and smiled pleasantly and nodded as the young man entered. He had a very strong face, with white hair hanging at the side, but was still a young man for one in such a high office. He was a man interested in many things, who could talk to men of any profession or to the mere man of pleasure, and could interest them in what he said, and force their respect and liking. And he was very good, and had, they said, seen much trouble.

"I am afraid I interrupted you," said the young man, tentatively.

"No, I have interrupted myself," replied the bishop. "I don't seem to make this clear to myself," he said, touching the paper in front of him, "and so I very much doubt if I am going to make it clear to any one else.

However," he added, smiling, as he pushed the manuscript to one side, "we are not going to talk about that now. What have you to tell me that is new?"

The younger man glanced up quickly at this, but the bishop's face showed that his words had had no ulterior meaning, and that he suspected nothing more serious to come than the gossip of the clubs or a report of the local political fight in which he was keenly interested, or on their mission on the East Side. But it seemed an opportunity to Latimer.

"I *have* something new to tell you," he said, gravely, and with his eyes turned toward the open fire, "and I don't know how to do it exactly. I mean I don't just know how it is generally done or how to tell it best." He hesitated and leaned forward, with his hands locked in front of him, and his elbows resting on his knees. He was not in the least frightened. The bishop had listened to many strange stories, to many confessions, in this same study, and had learned to take them as a matter of course; but to-night something in the manner of the young man before him made him stir uneasily, and he waited for him to disclose the object of his visit with some impatience.

"I will suppose, sir," said young Latimer, finally, "that you know me rather well - I mean you know who my people are, and what I am doing here in New York, and who my friends are, and what my work amounts to. You have let me see a great deal of you, and I have appreciated your doing so very much; to so young a man as myself it has been a great compliment, and it has been of great benefit to me. I know that better than any one else. I say this because unless you had shown me this confidence it would have been almost impossible for me to say to you what I am going to say now. But you have allowed me to come here frequently, and to see you and talk with you here in your study, and to see even more of your daughter. Of course, sir, you did not suppose that I came here only to see you. I came here because I found that if I did not see Miss Ellen for a day, that that day was wasted, and that I spent it uneasily and discontentedly, and the necessity of seeing her even more frequently has grown so great that I cannot come here as often as I seem to want to come unless I am engaged to her, unless I come as her husband that is to be." The young man had been speaking very slowly and picking his words, but now he raised his head and ran on quickly.

"I have spoken to her and told her how I love her, and she has told me that she loves me, and that if you will not oppose us, will marry me. That is the news I have to tell you, sir. I don't know but that I might have told it differently, but that is it. I need not urge on you my position and all that, because I do not think that weighs with you; but I do tell you that I love Ellen so dearly that, though I am not worthy of her, of course, I have no other pleasure than to give her pleasure and to try to make her happy. I have the power to do it; but what is much more, I have the wish to do it; it is all I think of now, and all that I can ever think of. What she thinks of me you must ask her; but what she is to me neither she can tell you nor do I believe that I myself could make you understand." The young man's face was flushed and eager, and as he finished speaking he raised his head and watched the bishop's countenance anxiously. But the older man's face was hidden by his hand as he leaned with his elbow on his writing-table. His other hand was playing with a pen, and when he began to speak, which he did after a long pause, he still turned it between his fingers and looked down at it.

"I suppose," he said, as softly as though he were speaking to himself, "that I should have known this; I suppose that I should have been better prepared to hear it. But it is one of those things which men put off - I mean those men who have children, put off - as they do making their wills, as something that is in the future and that may be shirked until it comes. We seem to think that our daughters will live with us always, just as we expect to live on ourselves until death comes one day and startles us and finds us unprepared." He took down his hand and smiled gravely at the younger man with an evident effort, and said, "I did not mean to speak so gloomily, but you see my point of view must be different from yours. And she says she loves you, does she?" he added, gently.

Young Latimer bowed his head and murmured something inarticulately in reply, and then held his head erect again and waited, still watching the bishop's face.

"I think she might have told me," said the older man; "but then I suppose this is the better way. I am young enough to understand that the old order changes, that the customs of my father's time differ from those of to-day. And there is no alternative, I suppose," he said, shaking his head. "I am stopped and told to deliver, and have no choice. I will get used to it in time," he went on, "but it seems very hard now. Fathers are selfish, I imagine, but she is all I have."

Young Latimer looked gravely into the fire and wondered how long it would last. He could just hear the piano from below, and he was anxious to return to her. And at the same time he was drawn toward the older man before him, and felt rather guilty, as though he really were robbing him. But at the bishop's next words he gave up any thought of a speedy release, and settled himself in his chair.

"We are still to have a long talk," said the bishop. "There are many things I must know, and of which I am sure you will inform me freely. I believe there are some who consider me hard, and even narrow on different points, but I do not think you will find me so, at least let us hope not. I must confess that for a moment I almost hoped that you might not be able to answer the questions I must ask you, but it was only for a moment. I am only too sure you will not be found wanting, and that the conclusion of our talk will satisfy us both. Yes, I am confident of that."

His manner changed, nevertheless, and Latimer saw that he was now facing a judge and not a plaintiff who had been robbed, and that he was in turn the defendant. And still he was in no way frightened.

"I like you," the bishop said, "I like you very much. As you say yourself, I have seen a great deal of you, because I have enjoyed your society, and your views and talk were good and young and fresh, and did me good. You have served to keep me in touch with the outside world, a world of which I used to know at one time a great deal. I know your people and I know you, I think, and many people have spoken to me of you. I see why now. They, no doubt, understood what was coming better than myself, and were meaning to reassure me concerning you. And they said nothing but what was good of you. But there are certain things of which no one can know but yourself, and concerning which no other person, save myself, has a right to question you. You have promised very fairly for my daughter's future; you have suggested more than you have said, but I understood. You can give her many pleasures which I have not been able to afford; she can get from you the means of seeing more of this world in which she lives, of meeting more people, and of indulging in her charities, or in her extravagances, for that matter, as she wishes. I have no fear of her bodily comfort; her life, as far as that is concerned, will be easier and broader, and with more power for good. Her future, as I say, as you say also, is assured; but I want to ask you this," the bishop leaned forward and watched the young man anxiously, "you can protect her in the future, but can you assure me that you can protect her from the past?"

Young Latimer raised his eyes calmly and said, "I don't think I quite understand."

"I have perfect confidence, I say," returned the bishop, "in you as far as your treatment of Ellen is concerned in the future. You love her and you would do everything to make the life of the woman you love a happy one; but this is it, Can you assure me that there is nothing in the past that may reach forward later and touch my daughter through you - no ugly story, no oats that have been sowed, and no boomerang that you have thrown wantonly and that has not returned - but which may return?"

"I think I understand you now, sir," said the young man, quietly. "I have lived," he began, "as other men of my sort have lived. You know what that is, for you must have seen it about you at college, and after that before you entered the Church. I judge so from your friends, who were your friends then, I understand. You know how they lived. I never went in for dissipation, if you mean that, because it never attracted me. I am afraid I kept out of it not so much out of respect for others as for respect for myself. I found my self-respect was a very good thing to keep, and I rather preferred keeping it and losing several pleasures that other men managed to enjoy, apparently with free consciences. I confess I used to rather envy them. It is no particular virtue on my part; the thing struck me as rather more vulgar than wicked, and so I have had no wild oats to speak of; and no woman, if that is what you mean, can write an anonymous letter, and no man can tell you a story about me that he could not tell in my presence."

There was something in the way the young man spoke which would have amply satisfied the outsider, had he been present; but the bishop's eyes were still unrelaxed and anxious. He made an impatient motion with his hand.

"I know you too well, I hope," he said, "to think of doubting your attitude in that particular. I know you are a gentleman, that is enough for that; but there is something beyond these more common evils. You see, I am terribly in earnest over this - you may think unjustly so, considering how well I know you, but this child is my only child. If her mother had lived, my responsibility would have been less great; but, as it is, God has left her here alone to me in my hands. I do not think He intended my duty should end when I had fed and clothed her, and taught her to read and write. I do not think He meant that I should only act as her guardian until the first man she fancied fancied her. I must look to her happiness not only now when she is

Richard Harding Davis

with me, but I must assure myself of it when she leaves my roof. These common sins of youth I acquit you of. Such things are beneath you, I believe, and I did not even consider them. But there are other toils in which men become involved, other evils or misfortunes which exist, and which threaten all men who are young and free and attractive in many ways to women, as well as men. You have lived the life of the young man of this day. You have reached a place in your profession when you can afford to rest and marry and assume the responsibilities of marriage. You look forward to a life of content and peace and honorable ambition - a life, with your wife at your side, which is to last forty or fifty years. You consider where you will be twenty years from now, at what point of your career you may become a judge or give up practice; your perspective is unlimited; you even think of the college to which you may send your son. It is a long, quiet future that you are looking forward to, and you choose my daughter as the companion for that future, as the one woman with whom you could live content for that length of time. And it is in that spirit that you come to me to-night and that you ask me for my daughter. Now I am going to ask you one question, and as you answer that I will tell you whether or not you can have Ellen for your wife. You look forward, as I say, to many years of life, and you have chosen her as best suited to live that period with you; but I ask you this, and I demand that you answer me truthfully, and that you remember that you are speaking to her father. Imagine that I had the power to tell you, or rather that some superhuman agent could convince you, that you had but a month to live, and that for what you did in that month you would not be held responsible either by any moral law or any law made by man, and that your life hereafter would not be influenced by your conduct in that month, would you spend it, I ask you - and on your answer depends mine - would you spend those thirty days, with death at the end, with my daughter, or with some other woman of whom I know nothing?"

Latimer sat for some time silent, until indeed, his silence assumed such a significance that he raised his head impatiently and said with a motion of the hand, "I mean to answer you in a minute; I want to be sure that I understand."

The bishop bowed his head in assent, and for a still longer period the men sat motionless. The clock in the corner seemed to tick more loudly, and the dead coals dropping in the grate had a sharp, aggressive sound. The notes of the piano that had risen from the room below had ceased.

"If I understand you," said Latimer, finally, and his voice and his face as he raised it were hard and aggressive, "you are stating a purely hypothetical case. You wish to try me by conditions which do not exist, which cannot exist. What justice is there, what right is there, in asking me to say how I would act under circumstances which are impossible, which lie beyond the limit of human experience? You cannot judge a man by what he would do if he were suddenly robbed of all his mental and moral training and of the habit of years. I am not admitting, understand me, that if the conditions which you suggest did exist that I would do one whit differently from what I will do if they remain as they are. I am merely denying your right to put such a question to me at all. You might just as well judge the shipwrecked sailors on a raft who eat each other's flesh as you would judge a sane, healthy man who did such a thing in his own home. Are you going to

Richard Harding Davis

condemn men who are ice-locked at the North Pole, or buried in the heart of Africa, and who have given up all thought of return and are half mad and wholly without hope, as you would judge ourselves? Are they to be weighed and balanced as you and I are, sitting here within the sound of the cabs outside and with a bake-shop around the corner? What you propose could not exist, could never happen. I could never be placed where I should have to make such a choice, and you have no right to ask me what I would do or how I would act under conditions that are super-human - you used the word yourself - where all that I have held to be good and just and true would be obliterated. I would be unworthy of myself, I would be unworthy of your daughter, if I considered such a state of things for a moment, or if I placed my hopes of marrying her on the outcome of such a test, and so, sir," said the young man, throwing back his head, "I must refuse to answer you."

The bishop lowered his hand from before his eyes and sank back wearily into his chair. "You have answered me," he said.

"You have no right to say that," cried the young man, springing to his feet. "You have no right to suppose anything or to draw any conclusions. I have not answered you." He stood with his head and shoulders thrown back, and with his hands resting on his hips and with the fingers working nervously at his waist.

"What you have said," replied the bishop, in a voice that had changed strangely, and which was inexpressibly sad and gentle, "is merely a curtain of words to cover up your true feeling. It would have been so easy to have said, 'For thirty days or for life Ellen is the only woman who has the power to make me happy.' You see that would have answered me and satisfied me. But you did not say that," he added, quickly, as the young man made a movement as if to speak.

"Well, and suppose this other woman did exist, what then?" demanded Latimer. "The conditions you suggest are impossible; you must, you will surely, sir, admit that."

"I do not know," replied the bishop, sadly; "I do not know. It may happen that whatever obstacle there has been which has kept you from her may be removed. It may be that she has married, it may be that she has fallen so low that you cannot marry her. But if you have loved her once, you may love her again; whatever it was that separated you in the past, that separates you now, that makes you prefer my daughter to her, may come to an end when you are married, when it will be too late, and when only trouble can come of it, and Ellen would bear that trouble. Can I risk that?"

"But I tell you it is impossible," cried the young man. "The woman is beyond the love of any man, at least such a man as I am, or try to be."

"Do you mean," asked the bishop, gently, and with an eager look of hope, "that she is dead?"

Latimer faced the father for some seconds in silence. Then he raised his head slowly. "No," he said, "I do not mean she is dead. No, she is not dead."

Again the bishop moved back wearily into his chair. "You mean then," he said, "perhaps, that she is a married woman?" Latimer pressed his lips together at

Richard Harding Davis

first as though he would not answer, and then raised his eyes coldly. "Perhaps," he said.

The older man had held up his hand as if to signify that what he was about to say should be listened to without interruption, when a sharp turning of the lock of the door caused both father and the suitor to start. Then they turned and looked at each other with anxious inquiry and with much concern, for they recognized for the first time that their voices had been loud. The older man stepped quickly across the floor, but before he reached the middle of the room the door opened from the outside, and his daughter stood in the door-way, with her head held down and her eyes looking at the floor.

"Ellen!" exclaimed the father, in a voice of pain and the deepest pity.

The girl moved toward the place from where his voice came, without raising her eyes, and when she reached him put her arms about him and hid her face on his shoulder. She moved as though she were tired, as though she were exhausted by some heavy work.

"My child," said the bishop, gently, "were you listening?" There was no reproach in his voice; it was simply full of pity and concern.

"I thought," whispered the girl, brokenly, "that he would be frightened; I wanted to hear what he would say. I thought I could laugh at him for it afterward. I did it for a joke. I thought -" she stopped with a little gasping sob that she tried to hide, and for a moment held herself erect and then sank back again into her father's arms with her head upon his breast.

Latimer started forward, holding out his arms to her. "Ellen," he said, "surely, Ellen, you are not against me. You see how preposterous it is, how unjust it is to me. You cannot mean -"

The girl raised her head and shrugged her shoulders slightly as though she were cold. "Father," she said, wearily, "ask him to go away, Why does he stay? Ask him to go away."

Latimer stopped and took a step back as though some one had struck him, and then stood silent with his face flushed and his eyes flashing. It was not in answer to anything that they said that he spoke, but to their attitude and what it suggested. "You stand there," he began, "you two stand there as though I were some-thing unclean, as though I had committed some crime. You look at me as though I were on trial for murder or worse. Both of you together against me. What have I done? What difference is there? You loved me a half-hour ago, Ellen; you said you did. I know you loved me; and you, sir," he added, more quietly, "treated me like a friend. Has anything come since then to change me or you? Be fair to me, be sensible. What is the use of this? It is a silly, needless, horrible mistake. You know I love you, Ellen; love you better than all the world. I don't have to tell you that; you know it, you can see and feel it. It does not need to be said; words can't make it any truer. You have confused yourselves and stultified yourselves with this trick, this test by hypothetical conditions, by considering what is not real or possible. It is simple enough; it is plain enough. You know I love you, Ellen, and you only, and that is all there is to it, and all that there is of any consequence in the world to me. The matter stops there; that is all there is for you to consider. Answer me, Ellen, speak to me.

Tell me that you believe me."

He stopped and moved a step toward her, but as he did so, the girl, still without looking up, drew herself nearer to her father and shrank more closely into his arms; but the father's face was troubled and doubtful, and he regarded the younger man with a look of the most anxious scrutiny. Latimer did not regard this. Their hands were raised against him as far as he could understand, and he broke forth again proudly, and with a defiant indignation:

"What right have you to judge me?" he began; "what do you know of what I have suffered, and endured, and overcome? How can you know what I have had to give up and put away from me? It's easy enough for you to draw your skirts around you, but what can a woman bred as you have been bred know of what I've had to fight against and keep under and cut away? It was an easy, beautiful idyl to you; your love came to you only when it should have come, and for a man who was good and worthy, and distinctly eligible - I don't mean that; forgive me, Ellen, but you drive me beside myself. But he is good and he believes himself worthy, and I say that myself before you both. But I am only worthy and only good because of that other love that I put away when it became a crime, when it became impossible. Do you know what it cost me? Do you know what it meant to me, and what I went through, and how I suffered? Do you know who this other woman is whom you are insulting with your doubts and guesses in the dark? Can't you spare her? Am I not enough? Perhaps it was easy for her, too; perhaps her silence cost her nothing; perhaps she did not suffer and has nothing but happiness and content to look forward to for the rest of her life; and I tell you that it is because we did put it away, and kill it, and not give way to it that I am whatever I am to-day; whatever good there is in me is due to that temptation and to the fact that I beat it and overcame it and kept myself honest and clean. And when I met you and learned to know you I believed in my heart that God had sent you to me that I might know what it was to love a woman whom I could marry and who could be my wife; that you were the reward for my having overcome temptation and the sign that I had done well. And now you throw me over and put me aside as though I were something low and unworthy, because of this temptation, because of this very thing that has made me know myself and my own strength and that has kept me up for you."

As the young man had been speaking, the bishop's eyes had never left his face, and as he finished, the face of the priest grew clearer and decided, and calmly exultant. And as Latimer ceased he bent his head above his daughter's, and said in a voice that seemed to speak with more than human inspiration. "My child," he said, "if God had given me a son I should have been proud if he could have spoken as this young man has done."

But the woman only said, "Let him go to her."

"Ellen, oh, Ellen!" cried the father.

He drew back from the girl in his arms and looked anxiously and feelingly at her lover. "How could you, Ellen," he said, "how could you?" He was watching the young man's face with eyes full of sympathy and concern. "How little you know him," he said, "how little you understand. He will not do that," he added quickly, but looking questioningly at Latimer and speaking in a tone almost of command. "He will not undo all that he has done; I know him better than that." But Latimer made no answer, and for a moment the two men stood watching each other and questioning each other with their eyes. Then Latimer turned, and without again so much as glancing at the girl walked steadily to the door and left the room. He passed on slowly down the stairs and out into the night, and paused upon the top of the steps leading to the street. Below him lay the avenue with its double line of lights stretching off in two long perspectives. The lamps of hundreds of cabs and carriages flashed as they advanced toward him and shone for a moment at the turnings of the cross-streets, and from either side came the ceaseless rush and murmur, and over all hung the strange mystery that covers a great city at night. Latimer's rooms lay to the south, but he stood looking toward a spot to the north with a reckless, harassed look in his face that had not been there for many months. He stood so for a minute, and then gave a short shrug of disgust at his momentary doubt and ran quickly down the steps. "No," he said, "if it were for a month, yes; but it is to be for many years, many more long years." And turning his back resolutely to the north he went slowly home.

THE TRAILER FOR ROOM NO. 8

The "trailer" for the green-goods men who rented room No. 8 in Case's tenement had had no work to do for the last few days, and was cursing his luck in consequence.

He was entirely too young to curse, but he had never been told so, and, indeed, so imperfect had his training been that he had never been told not to do anything as long as it pleased him to do it and made existence any more bearable.

He had been told when he was very young, before the man and woman who had brought him into the world had separated, not to crawl out on the fire-escape, because he might break his neck, and later, after his father had walked off Hegelman's Slip into the East River while very drunk, and his mother had been sent to the penitentiary for grand larceny, he had been told not to let the police catch him sleeping under the bridge.

With these two exceptions he had been told to do as he pleased, which was the very mockery of advice, as he was just about as well able to do as he pleased as is any one who has to beg or steal what he eats and has to sleep in hall-ways or over the iron gratings of warm cellars and has the officers of the children's societies always after him to put him in a "Home" and make him be "good."

"Snipes," as the trailer was called, was determined no one should ever force him to be good if he could possibly prevent it. And he certainly did do a great deal to prevent it. He knew what having to be good meant. Some of the boys who had escaped from the Home had told him all about that. It meant wearing shoes and a blue and white checkered apron, and making cane-bottomed chairs all day, and having to wash yourself in a big iron tub twice a week, not to speak of having to move about like machines whenever the lady teacher hit a bell. So when the green-goods men, of whom the genial Mr. Alf Wolfe was the chief, asked Snipes to act as "trailer" for them at a quarter of a dollar for every victim he shadowed, he jumped at the offer and was proud of the position.

If you should happen to keep a grocery store in the country, or to run the village post-office, it is not unlikely that you know what a green-goods man is; but in case you don't, and have only a vague idea as to how he lives, a paragraph of explanation must be inserted here for your particular benefit. Green goods is the technical name for counterfeit bills, and the green-goods men send out circulars to countrymen all over the United States, offering to sell them $5,000 worth of counterfeit money for $500, and ease their conscience by explaining to them that by purchasing these green goods they are hurting no one but the Government, which is quite able, with its big surplus, to stand the loss. They enclose a letter which is to serve their victim as a mark of identification or credential when he comes on to purchase.

The address they give him is in one of the many

drug-store and cigar-store post-offices which are scattered all over New York, and which contribute to make vice and crime so easy that the evil they do cannot be reckoned in souls lost or dollars stolen. If the letter from the countryman strikes the dealers in green goods as sincere, they appoint an interview with him by mail in rooms they rent for the purpose, and if they, on meeting him there, think he is still in earnest and not a detective or officer in disguise, they appoint still another interview, to be held later in the day in the back room of some saloon.

Then the countryman is watched throughout the day from the moment he leaves the first meeting-place until he arrives at the saloon. If anything in his conduct during that time leads the man whose duty it is to follow him, or the "trailer," as the profession call it, to believe he is a detective, he finds when he arrives at the saloon that there is no one to receive him. But if the trailer regards his conduct as unsuspicious, he is taken to another saloon, not the one just appointed, which is, perhaps, a most respectable place, but to the thieves' own private little rendezvous, where he is robbed in any of the several different ways best suited to their purpose.

Snipes was a very good trailer. He was so little that no one ever noticed him, and he could keep a man in sight no matter how big the crowd was, or how rapidly it changed and shifted. And he was as patient as he was quick, and would wait for hours if needful, with his eye on a door, until his man reissued into the street again. And if the one he shadowed looked behind him to see if he was followed, or dodged up and down different streets, as if he were trying to throw off pursuit, or despatched a note or telegram, or stopped to speak to a policeman or any special officer, as a detective might, who thought he had his men safely in hand, off Snipes would go on a run, to where Alf Wolfe was waiting, and tell what he had seen.

Then Wolfe would give him a quarter or more, and the trailer would go back to his post opposite Case's tenement, and wait for another victim to issue forth, and for the signal from No. 8 to follow him. It was not much fun, and "customers," as Mr. Wolfe always called them, had been scarce, and Mr. Wolfe, in consequence, had been cross and nasty in his temper, and had batted Snipe out of the way on more than one occasion. So the trailer was feeling blue and disconsolate, and wondered how it was that "Naseby" Raegen, "Rags" Raegen's younger brother, had had the luck to get a two weeks' visit to the country with the Fresh Air Fund children, while he had not.

He supposed it was because Naseby had sold papers, and wore shoes, and went to night school, and did many other things equally objectionable. Still, what Naseby had said about the country, and riding horse-back, and the fishing, and the shooting crows with no cops to stop you, and watermelons for nothing, had sounded wonderfully attractive and quite improbable, except that it was one of Naseby's peculiarly sneaking ways to tell the truth. Anyway, Naseby had left Cherry Street for good, and had gone back to the country to work there. This all helped to make Snipes morose, and it was with a cynical smile of satisfaction that he watched an old countryman coming slowly up the street, and asking his way timidly of the Italians to Case's tenement.

The countryman looked up and about him in evident

bewilderment and anxiety. He glanced hesitatingly across at the boy leaning against the wall of a saloon, but the boy was watching two sparrows fighting in the dirt of the street, and did not see him. At least, it did not look as if he saw him. Then the old man knocked on the door of Case's tenement. No one came, for the people in the house had learned to leave inquiring countrymen to the gentleman who rented room No. 8, and as that gentleman was occupied at that moment with a younger countryman, he allowed the old man, whom he had first cautiously observed from the top of the stairs, to remain where he was.

The old man stood uncertainly on the stoop, and then removed his heavy black felt hat and rubbed his bald head and the white shining locks of hair around it with a red bandanna handkerchief. Then he walked very slowly across the street toward Snipes, for the rest of the street was empty, and there was no one else at hand. The old man was dressed in heavy black broadcloth, quaintly cut, with boot legs showing up under the trousers, and with faultlessly clean linen of home-made manufacture.

"I can't make the people in that house over there hear me," complained the old man, with the simple confidence that old age has in very young boys. "Do you happen to know if they're at home?"

"Nop," growled Snipes.

"I'm looking for a man named Perceval," said the stranger; "he lives in that house, and I wanter see him on most particular business. It isn't a very pleasing place he lives in, is it - at least," he hurriedly added, as if fearful of giving offence, "it isn't much on the outside? Do you happen to know him?"

Perceval was Alf Wolfe's business name.

"Nop," said the trailer.

"Well, I'm not looking for him," explained the stranger, slowly, "as much as I'm looking for a young man that I kind of suspect is been to see him to-day: a young man that looks like me, only younger. Has lightish hair and pretty tall and lanky, and carrying a shiny black bag with him. Did you happen to hev noticed him going into that place across the way?"

"Nop," said Snipes.

The old man sighed and nodded his head thoughtfully at Snipes, and puckered up the corners of his mouth, as though he were thinking deeply. He had wonderfully honest blue eyes, and with the white hair hanging around his sun-burned face, he looked like an old saint. But the trailer didn't know that: he did know, though, that this man was a different sort from the rest. Still, that was none of his business.

"What is't you want to see him about?" he asked sullenly, while he looked up and down the street and everywhere but at the old man, and rubbed one bare foot slowly over the other.

The old man looked pained, and much to Snipe's surprise, the question brought the tears to his eyes, and his lips trembled. Then he swerved slightly, so that he might have fallen if Snipes had not caught him and helped him across the pavement to a seat on a stoop. "Thankey, son," said the stranger; "I'm not as strong as

I was, an' the sun's mighty hot, an' these streets of yours smell mighty bad, and I've had a powerful lot of trouble these last few days. But if I could see this man Perceval before my boy does, I know I could fix it, and it would all come out right."

"What do you want to see him about?" repeated the trailer, suspiciously, while he fanned the old man with his hat. Snipes could not have told you why he did this or why this particular old countryman was any different from the many others who came to buy counterfeit money and who were thieves at heart as well as in deed.

"I want to see him about my son," said the old man to the little boy. "He's a bad man whoever he is. This 'ere Perceval is a bad man. He sends down his wickedness to the country and tempts weak folks to sin. He teaches 'em ways of evil-doing they never heard of, and he's ruined my son with the others - ruined him. I've had nothing to do with the city and its ways; we're strict living, simple folks, and perhaps we've been too strict, or Abraham wouldn't have run away to the city. But I thought it was best, and I doubted nothing when the fresh-air children came to the farm. I didn't like city children, but I let 'em come. I took 'em in, and did what I could to make it pleasant for 'em. Poor little fellers, all as thin as corn-stalks and pale as ghosts, and as dirty as you.

"I took 'em in and let 'em ride the horses, and swim in the river, and shoot crows in the cornfield, and eat all the cherries they could pull, and what did the city send me in return for that? It sent me this thieving, rascally scheme of this man Perceval's, and it turned my boy's head, and lost him to me. I saw him poring over the note and reading it as if it were Gospel, and I suspected nothing. And when he asked me if he could keep it, I said yes he could, for I thought he wanted it for a curiosity, and then off he put with the black bag and the $200 he's been saving up to start housekeeping with when the old Deacon says he can marry his daughter Kate." The old man placed both hands on his knees and went on excitedly.

"The old Deacon says he'll not let 'em marry till Abe has $2,000, and that is what the boy's come after. He wants to buy $2,000 worth of bad money with his $200 worth of good money, to show the Deacon, just as though it were likely a marriage after such a crime as that would ever be a happy one."

Snipes had stopped fanning the old man, as he ran on, and was listening intently, with an uncomfortable feeling of sympathy and sorrow, uncomfortable because he was not used to it.

He could not see why the old man should think the city should have treated his boy better because he had taken care of the city's children, and he was puzzled between his allegiance to the gang and his desire to help the gang's innocent victim, and then because he was an innocent victim and not a "customer," he let his sympathy get the better of his discretion.

"Saay," he began, abruptly, "I'm not sayin' nothin' to nobody, and nobody's sayin' nothin' to me - see? but I guess your son'll be around here to-day, sure. He's got to come before one, for this office closes sharp at one, and we goes home. Now, I've got the call whether he gets his stuff taken off him or whether the boys leave him alone. If I say the word, they'd no more come near him than if he had the cholera - see? An' I'll say it for this oncet, just for you. Hold on," he commanded, as the old man raised his voice in surprised interrogation, "don't ask no questions, 'cause you won't get no answers 'except lies. You find your way back to the Grand Central Depot and wait there, and I'll steer your son down to you, sure, as soon as I can find him - see? Now get along, or you'll get me inter trouble."

"You've been lying to me, then," cried the old man, "and you're as bad as any of them, and my boy's over in that house now."

He scrambled up from the stoop, and before the trailer could understand what he proposed to do, had dashed across the street and up the stoop, and up the stairs, and had burst into room No. 8.

Snipes tore after him. "Come back! come back out of that, you old fool!" he cried. "You'll get killed in there!" Snipes was afraid to enter room No. 8, but he could hear from the outside the old man challenging Alf Wolfe in a resonant angry voice that rang through the building.

"Whew!" said Snipes, crouching on the stairs, "there's goin' to be a muss this time, sure!"

"Where's my son? Where have you hidden my son?" demanded, the old man. He ran across the room and pulled open a door that led into another room, but it was empty. He had fully expected to see his boy murdered and quartered, and with his pockets inside out. He turned on Wolfe, shaking his white hair like a mane. "Give me up my son, you rascal you!" he cried, "or I'll get the police, and I'll tell them how you decoy honest boys to your den and murder them."

"Are you drunk or crazy, or just a little of both?" asked Mr. Wolfe. "For a cent I'd throw you out of that window. Get out of here! Quick, now! You're too old to get excited like that; it's not good for you."

But this only exasperated the old man the more, and he made a lunge at the confidence man's throat. Mr. Wolfe stepped aside and caught him around the waist and twisted his leg around the old man's rheumatic one, and held him. "Now," said Wolfe, as quietly as though he were giving a lesson in wrestling, "if I wanted to, I could break your back."

The old man glared up at him, panting. "Your son's not here," said Wolfe, "and this is a private gentleman's private room. I could turn you over to the police for assault if I wanted to; but," he added, magnanimously, "I won't. Now get out of here and go home to your wife, and when you come to see the sights again don't drink so much raw whiskey." He half carried the old farmer to the top of the stairs and dropped him, and went back and closed the door. Snipes came up and helped him down and out, and the old man and the boy walked slowly and in silence out to the Bowery. Snipes helped his companion into a car and put him off at the Grand Central Depot. The heat and the excitement had told heavily on the old man, and he seemed dazed and beaten.

He was leaning on the trailer's shoulder and waiting for his turn in the line in front of the ticket window, when a tall, gawky, good-looking country lad sprang out of it and at him with an expression of surprise and anxiety.

"Father," he said, "father, what's wrong? What are you doing here? Is anybody ill at home? Are *you* ill?"

"Abraham," said the old man, simply, and dropped heavily on the younger man's shoulder. Then he raised his head sternly and said: "I thought you were murdered, but better that than a thief, Abraham. What brought you here? What did you do with that rascal's letter? What did you do with his money?"

The trailer drew cautiously away; the conversation was becoming unpleasantly personal.

"I don't know what you're talking about," said Abraham, calmly. "The Deacon gave his consent the other night without the $2,000, and I took the $200 I'd saved and came right on in the fust train to buy the ring. It's pretty, isn't it?" he said, flushing, as he pulled out a little velvet box and opened it.

The old man was so happy at this that he laughed and cried alternately, and then he made a grab for the trailer and pulled him down beside him on one of the benches.

"You've got to come with me," he said, with kind severity. "You're a good boy, but your folks have let you run wrong. You've been good to me, and you said you would get me back my boy and save him from those thieves, and I believe now that you meant it. Now you're just coming back with us to the farm and the cows and the river, and you can eat all you want and live with us, and never, never see this unclean, wicked city again."

Snipes looked up keenly from under the rim of his hat

and rubbed one of his muddy feet over the other as was his habit. The young countryman, greatly puzzled, and the older man smiling kindly, waited expectantly in silence. From outside came the sound of the car-bells jangling, and the rattle of cabs, and the cries of drivers, and all the varying rush and turmoil of a great metropolis. Green fields, and running rivers, and fruit that did not grow in wooden boxes or brown paper cones, were myths and idle words to Snipes, but this "unclean, wicked city" he knew.

"I guess you're too good for me," he said, with an uneasy laugh. "I guess little old New York's good enough for me."

"What!" cried the old man, in the tones of greatest concern. "You would go back to that den of iniquity, surely not, - to that thief Perceval?"

"Well," said the trailer, slowly, "and he's not such a bad lot, neither. You see he could hev broke your neck that time when you was choking him, but he didn't. There's your train," he added hurriedly and jumping away. "Good-by. So long, old man. I'm much 'bliged to you jus' for asking me."

Two hours later the farmer and his son were making the family weep and laugh over their adventures, as they all sat together on the porch with the vines about it; and the trailer was leaning against the wall of a saloon and apparently counting his ten toes, but in reality watching for Mr. Wolfe to give the signal from the window of room No. 8.

"THERE WERE NINETY AND NINE"

Young Harringford, or the "Goodwood Plunger," as he was perhaps better known at that time, had come to Monte Carlo in a very different spirit and in a very different state of mind from any in which he had ever visited the place before. He had come there for the same reason that a wounded lion, or a poisoned rat, for that matter, crawls away into a corner, that it may be alone when it dies. He stood leaning against one of the pillars of the Casino with his back to the moonlight, and with his eyes blinking painfully at the flaming lamps above the green tables inside. He knew they would be put out very soon; and as he had something to do then, he regarded them fixedly with painful earnestness, as a man who is condemned to die at sunrise watches through his barred windows for the first gray light of the morning.

That queer, numb feeling in his head and the sharp line of pain between his eyebrows which had been growing worse for the last three weeks, was troubling him more terribly than ever before, and his nerves had thrown off all control and rioted at the base of his head and at his wrists, and jerked and twitched as though, so it seemed to him, they were striving to pull the tired body into pieces and to set themselves free. He was wondering whether if he should take his hand from his pocket and touch his head he would find that it had grown longer,

Richard Harding Davis

and had turned into a soft, spongy mass which would give beneath his fingers. He considered this for some time, and even went so far as to half withdraw one hand, but thought better of it and shoved it back again as he considered how much less terrible it was to remain in doubt than to find that this phenomenon had actually taken place.

The pity of the whole situation was, that the boy was only a boy with all his man's miserable knowledge of the world, and the reason of it all was, that he had entirely too much heart and not enough money to make an unsuccessful gambler. If he had only been able to lose his conscience instead of his money, or even if he had kept his conscience and won, it is not likely that he would have been waiting for the lights to go out at Monte Carlo. But he had not only lost all of his money and more besides, which he could never make up, but he had lost other things which meant much more to him now than money, and which could not be made up or paid back at even usurious interest. He had not only lost the right to sit at his father's table, but the right to think of the girl whose place in Surrey ran next to that of his own people, and whose lighted window in the north wing he had watched on those many dreary nights when she had been ill, from his own terrace across the trees in the park. And all he had gained was the notoriety that made him a by-word with decent people, and the hero of the race-tracks and the music-halls. He was no longer "Young Harringford, the eldest son of the Harringfords of Surrey," but the "Goodwood Plunger," to whom Fortune had made desperate love and had then jilted, and mocked, and overthrown.

As he looked back at it now and remembered himself as he was then, it seemed as though he was considering an entirely distinct and separate personage - a boy of whom he liked to think, who had had strong, healthy ambitions and gentle tastes. He reviewed it passionlessly as he stood staring at the lights inside the Casino, as clearly as he was capable of doing in his present state and with miserable interest. How he had laughed when young Norton told him in boyish confidence that there was a horse named Siren in his father's stables which would win the Goodwood Cup; how, having gone down to see Norton's people when the long vacation began, he had seen Siren daily, and had talked of her until two every morning in the smoking-room, and had then staid up two hours later to watch her take her trial spin over the downs. He remembered how they used to stamp back over the long grass wet with dew, comparing watches and talking of the time in whispers, and said good night as the sun broke over the trees in the park. And then just at this time of all others, when the horse was the only interest of those around him, from Lord Norton and his whole household down to the youngest stable-boy and oldest gaffer in the village, he had come into his money.

And then began the then and still inexplicable plunge into gambling, and the wagering of greater sums than the owner of Siren dared to risk himself, the secret backing of the horse through commissioners all over England, until the boy by his single fortune had brought the odds against her from 60 to 0 down to 6 to 0. He recalled, with a thrill that seemed to settle his nerves for the moment, the little black specks at the starting-post and the larger specks as the horses turned the first corner. The rest of the people on the coach were making a great deal of noise, he remembered, but he, who had more to lose than any one or all of them

Richard Harding Davis

together, had stood quite still with his feet on the wheel and his back against the box-seat, and with his hands sunk into his pockets and the nails cutting through his gloves. The specks grew into horses with bits of color on them, and then the deep muttering roar of the crowd merged into one great shout, and swelled and grew into sharper, quicker, impatient cries, as the horses turned into the stretch with only their heads showing toward the goal. Some of the people were shouting "Firefly!" and others were calling on "Vixen!" and others, who had their glasses up, cried "Trouble leads!" but he only waited until he could distinguish the Norton colors, with his lips pressed tightly together. Then they came so close that their hoofs echoed as loudly as when horses gallop over a bridge, and from among the leaders Siren's beautiful head and shoulders showed like sealskin in the sun, and the boy on her back leaned forward and touched her gently with his hand, as they had so often seen him do on the downs, and Siren, as though he had touched a spring, leaped forward with her head shooting back and out, like a piston-rod that has broken loose from its fastening and beats the air, while the jockey sat motionless, with his right arm hanging at his side as limply as though it were broken, and with his left moving forward and back in time with the desperate strokes of the horse's head.

"Siren wins!" cried Lord Norton, with a grim smile, and "Siren!" the mob shouted back with wonder and angry disappointment, and "Siren!" the hills echoed from far across the course. Young Harringford felt as if he had suddenly been lifted into heaven after three months of purgatory, and smiled uncertainly at the excited people on the coach about him. It made him smile even now when he recalled young Norton's flushed face and the awe and reproach in his voice when he climbed up and whispered, "Why, Cecil, they say in the ring you've won a fortune, and you never told us." And how Griffith, the biggest of the bookmakers, with the rest of them at his back, came up to him and touched his hat resentfully, and said, "You'll have to give us time, sir; I'm very hard hit"; and how the crowd stood about him and looked at him curiously, and the Certain Royal Personage turned and said, "Who - not that boy, surely?" Then how, on the day following, the papers told of the young gentleman who of all others had won a fortune, thousands and thousands of pounds they said, getting back sixty for every one he had ventured; and pictured him in baby clothes with the cup in his arms, or in an Eton jacket; and how all of them spoke of him slightingly, or admiringly, as the "Goodwood Plunger."

He did not care to go on after that; to recall the mortification of his father, whose pride was hurt and whose hopes were dashed by this sudden, mad freak of fortune, nor how he railed at it and provoked him until the boy rebelled and went back to the courses, where he was a celebrity and a king.

The rest is a very common story. Fortune and greater fortune at first; days in which he could not lose, days in which he drove back to the crowded inns choked with dust, sunburnt and fagged with excitement, to a riotous supper and baccarat, and afterward went to sleep only to see cards and horses and moving crowds and clouds of dust; days spent in a short covert coat, with a field-glass over his shoulder and with a pasteboard ticket dangling from his buttonhole; and then came the change that brought conscience up again, and the visits to the Jews, and the slights of the men who had never been his friends, but whom he had thought had at least liked him for himself, even if he did not like them; and then debts, and more debts, and the borrowing of money to pay here and there, and threats of executions; and, with it all, the longing for the fields and trout springs of Surrey and the walk across the park to where she lived.

This grew so strong that he wrote to his father, and was told briefly that he who was to have kept up the family name had dragged it into the dust of the race-courses, and had changed it at his own wish to that of the Boy Plunger - and that the breach was irreconcilable.

Then this queer feeling came on, and he wondered why he could not eat, and why he shivered even when the room was warm or the sun shining, and the fear came upon him that with all this trouble and disgrace his head might give way, and then that it had given way. This came to him at all times, and lately more frequently and with a fresher, more cruel thrill of terror, and he began to watch himself and note how he spoke, and to repeat over what he had said to see if it were sensible, and to question himself as to why he laughed, and at what. It was not a question of whether it would or would not be cowardly; It was simply a necessity. The thing had to be stopped. He had to have rest and sleep and peace again. He had boasted in those reckless, prosperous days that if by any possible chance he should lose his money he would drive a hansom, or emigrate to the colonies, or take the shilling. He had no patience in those days with men who could not live on in adversity, and who were found in the gun-room with a hole in their heads, and whose family asked their polite friends to believe that a man used to firearms from his school-days had tried to load a hair-trigger revolver with the muzzle pointed at his forehead. He had expressed a fine contempt for those men then, but now he had forgotten all that, and thought only of the relief it would bring, and not how others might suffer by it. If he did consider this, it was only to conclude that they would quite understand, and be glad that his pain and fear were over.

Then he planned a grand *coup* which was to pay off all his debts and give him a second chance to present himself a supplicant at his father's house. If it failed, he would have to stop this queer feeling in his head at once. The Grand Prix and the English horse was the final *coup*. On this depended everything - the return of his fortunes, the reconciliation with his father, and the possibility of meeting her again. It was a very hot day he remembered, and very bright; but the tall poplars on the road to the races seemed to stop growing just at a level with his eyes. Below that it was clear enough, but all above seemed black - as though a cloud had fallen and was hanging just over the people's heads. He thought of speaking of this to his man Walters, who had followed his fortunes from the first, but decided not to do so, for, as it was, he had noticed that Walters had observed him closely of late, and had seemed to spy upon him. The race began, and he looked through his glass for the English horse in the front and could not find her, and the Frenchman beside him cried, "Frou Frou!" as Frou Frou passed the goal. He lowered his glasses slowly and unscrewed them very carefully before dropping them back into the case; then he buckled the strap, and turned and looked about him. Two Frenchmen who had won a hundred francs between them were jumping and dancing at his side. He remembered wondering why they did not speak in English. Then the sunlight changed to a yellow, nasty glare, as though a calcium light had been turned on the

Richard Harding Davis

glass and colors, and he pushed his way back to his carriage, leaning heavily on the servant's arm, and drove slowly back to Paris, with the driver flecking his horses fretfully with his whip, for he had wished to wait and see the end of the races.

He had selected Monte Carlo as the place for it, because it was more unlike his home than any other spot, and because one summer night, when he had crossed the lawn from the Casino to the hotel with a gay party of young men and women, they had come across something under a bush which they took to be a dog or a man asleep, and one of the men had stepped forward and touched it with his foot, and had then turned sharply and said, "Take those girls away"; and while some hurried the women back, frightened and curious, he and the others had picked up the body and found it to be that of a young Russian whom they had just seen losing, with a very bad grace, at the tables. There was no passion in his face now, and his evening dress was quite unruffled, and only a black spot on the shirt front showed where the powder had burnt the linen. It had made a great impression on him then, for he was at the height of his fortunes, with crowds of sycophantic friends and a retinue of dependents at his heels. And now that he was quite alone and disinherited by even these sorry companions there seemed no other escape from the pain in his brain but to end it, and he sought this place of all others as the most fitting place in which to die.

So, after Walters had given the proper papers and checks to the commissioner who handled his debts for him, he left Paris and took the first train for Monte Carlo, sitting at the window of the carriage, and beating a nervous tattoo on the pane with his ring until the old gentleman at the other end of the compartment scowled at him. But Harringford did not see him, nor the trees and fields as they swept by, and it was not until Walters came and said, "You get out here, sir," that he recognized the yellow station and the great hotels on the hill above. It was half-past eleven, and the lights in the Casino were still burning brightly. He wondered whether he would have time to go over to the hotel and write a letter to his father and to her. He decided, after some difficult consideration, that he would not. There was nothing to say that they did not know already, or that they would fail to understand. But this suggested to him that what they had written to him must be destroyed at once, before any stranger could claim the right to read it. He took his letters from his pocket and looked them over carefully. They were most unpleasant reading. They all seemed to be about money; some begged to remind him of this or that debt, of which he had thought continuously for the last month, while others were abusive and insolent. Each of them gave him actual pain. One was the last letter he had received from his father just before leaving Paris, and though he knew it by heart, he read it over again for the last time. That it came too late, that it asked what he knew now to be impossible, made it none the less grateful to him, but that it offered peace and a welcome home made it all the more terrible.

"I came to take this step through young Hargraves, the new curate," his father wrote, "though he was but the instrument in the hands of Providence. He showed me the error of my conduct toward you, and proved to me that my duty and the inclination of my heart were toward the same end. He read this morning for the second lesson the story of the Prodigal Son, and I heard it without recognition and with no present application until he came to the verse which tells how the father came to his son 'when he was yet a great way off.' He saw him, it says, 'when he was yet a great way off,' and ran to meet him. He did not wait for the boy to knock at his gate and beg to be let in, but went out to meet him, and took him in his arms and led him back to his home. Now, my boy, my son, it seems to me as if you had never been so far off from me as you are at this present time, as if you had never been so greatly separated from me in every thought and interest; we are even worse than strangers, for you think that my hand is against you, that I have closed the door of your home to you and driven you away. But what I have done I beg of you to forgive: to forget what I may have said in the past, and only to think of what I say now. Your brothers are good boys and have been good sons to me, and God knows I am thankful for such sons, and thankful to them for bearing themselves as they have done.

"But, my boy, my first-born, my little Cecil, they can never be to me what you have been. I can never feel for them as I feel for you; they are the ninety and nine who have never wandered away upon the mountains, and who have never been tempted, and have never left their home for either good or evil. But you, Cecil, though you have made my heart ache until I thought and even hoped it would stop beating, and though you have given me many, many nights that I could not sleep, are still dearer to me than anything else in the world. You are the flesh of my flesh and the bone of my bone, and I cannot bear living on without you. I cannot be at rest here, or look forward contentedly to a rest hereafter, unless you are by me and hear me, unless I can see your face and touch you and hear your laugh in the halls. Come back to me, Cecil; to

Harring-ford and the people that know you best, and know what is best in you and love you for it. I can have only a few more years here now when you will take my place and keep up my name. I will not be here to trouble you much longer; but, my boy, while I am here, come to me and make me happy for the rest of my life. There are others who need you, Cecil. You know whom I mean. I saw her only yesterday, and she asked me of you with such splendid disregard for what the others standing by might think, and as though she dared me or them to say or even imagine anything against you. You cannot keep away from us both much longer. Surely not; you will come back and make us happy for the rest of our lives."

The Goodwood Plunger turned his back to the lights so that the people passing could not see his face, and tore the letter up slowly and dropped it piece by piece over the balcony. "If I could," he whispered; "if I could." The pain was a little worse than usual just then, but it was no longer a question of inclination. He felt only this desire to stop these thoughts and doubts and the physical tremor that shook him. To rest and sleep, that was what he must have, and peace. There was no peace at home or anywhere else while this thing lasted. He could not see why they worried him in this way. It was quite impossible. He felt much more sorry for them than for himself, but only because they could not understand. He was quite sure that if they could feel what he suffered they would help him, even to end it.

He had been standing for some time with his back to the light, but now he turned to face it and to take up his watch again. He felt quite sure the lights would not burn much longer. As he turned, a woman came forward from out the lighted hall, hovered uncertainly before him, and then made a silent salutation, which was something between a courtesy and a bow. That she was a woman and rather short and plainly dressed, and that her bobbing up and down annoyed him, was all that he realized of her presence, and he quite failed to connect her movements with himself in any way. "Sir," she said in French, "I beg your pardon, but might I speak with you?" The Goodwood Plunger possessed a somewhat various knowledge of Monte Carlo and its *habitues*. It was not the first time that women who had lost at the tables had begged a napoleon from him, or asked the distinguished child of fortune what color or combination she should play. That, in his luckier days, had happened often and had amused him, but now he moved back irritably and wished that the figure in front of him would disappear as it had come.

"I am in great trouble, sir," the woman said. "I have no friends here, sir, to whom I may apply. I am very bold, but my anxiety is very great."

The Goodwood Plunger raised his hat slightly and bowed. Then he concentrated his eyes with what was a distinct effort on the queer little figure hovering in front of him, and stared very hard. She wore an odd piece of red coral for a brooch, and by looking steadily at this he brought the rest of the figure into focus and saw, without surprise, - for every commonplace seemed strange to him now, and everything peculiar quite a matter of course, - that she was distinctly not an *habituee* of the place, and looked more like a lady's maid than an adventuress. She was French and pretty, - such a girl as might wait in a Duval restaurant or sit as a cashier behind a little counter near the door.

"We should not be here," she said, as if in answer to

his look and in apology for her presence. "But Louis, my husband, he would come. I told him that this was not for such as we are, but Louis is so bold. He said that upon his marriage tour he would live with the best, and so here he must come to play as the others do. We have been married, sir, only since Tuesday, and we must go back to Paris to-morrow; they would give him only the three days. He is not a gambler; he plays dominos at the cafes, it is true. But what will you? He is young and with so much spirit, and I know that you, sir, who are so fortunate and who understand so well how to control these tables, I know that you will persuade him. He will not listen to me; he is so greatly excited and so little like himself. You will help me, sir, will you not? You will speak to him?"

The Goodwood Plunger knit his eyebrows and closed the lids once or twice, and forced the mistiness and pain out of his eyes. It was most annoying. The woman seemed to be talking a great deal and to say very much, but he could not make sense of it. He moved his shoulders slightly. "I can't understand," he said wearily, turning away.

"It is my husband," the woman said anxiously: "Louis, he is playing at the table inside, and he is only an apprentice to old Carbut the baker, but he owns a third of the store. It was my *dot* that paid for it," she added proudly. "Old Carbut says he may have it all for 20,000 francs, and then old Carbut will retire, and we will be proprietors. We have saved a little, and we had counted to buy the rest in five or six years if we were very careful."

"I see, I see," said the Plunger, with a little short laugh of relief; "I understand." He was greatly comforted to think that it was not so bad as it had threatened. He saw her distinctly now and followed what she said quite easily, and even such a small matter as talking with this woman seemed to help him.

"He is gambling," he said, "and losing the money, and you come to me to advise him what to play. I understand. Well, tell him he will lose what little he has left; tell him I advise him to go home; tell him -"

"No, no!" the girl said excitedly; "you do not understand; he has not lost, he has won. He has won, oh, so many rolls of money, but he will not stop. Do you not see? He has won as much as we could earn in many months - in many years, sir, by saving and working, oh, so very hard! And now he risks it again, and I cannot force him away. But if you, sir, if you would tell him how great the chances are against him, if you who know would tell him how foolish he is not to be content with what he has, he would listen. He says to me, 'Bah! you are a woman'; and he is so red and fierce; he is imbecile with the sight of the money, but he will listen to a grand gentleman like you. He thinks to win more and more, and he thinks to buy another third from old Carbut. Is it not foolish? It is so wicked of him."

"Oh, yes," said the Goodwood Plunger, nodding, "I see now. You want me to take him away so that he can keep what he has. I see; but I don't know him. He will not listen to me, you know; I have no right to interfere."

He turned away, rubbing his hand across his forehead. He wished so much that this woman would leave him by himself.

"Ah, but, sir," cried the girl, desperately, and touching his coat, "you who are so fortunate, and so rich, and of the great world, you cannot feel what this is to me. To have my own little shop and to be free, and not to slave, and sew, and sew until my back and fingers burn with the pain. Speak to him, sir; ah, speak to him! It is so easy a thing to do, and he will listen to you."

The Goodwood Plunger turned again abruptly. "Where is he?" he said. "Point him out to me."

The woman ran ahead, with a murmur of gratitude, to the open door and pointed to where her husband was standing leaning over and placing some money on one of the tables. He was a handsome young Frenchman, as *bourgeois* as his wife, and now terribly alive and excited. In the self-contained air of the place and in contrast with the silence of the great hall he seemed even more conspicuously out of place. The Plunger touched him on the arm, and the Frenchman shoved the hand off impatiently and without looking around. The Plunger touched him again and forced him to turn toward him.

"Well!" said the Frenchman, quickly. "Well?"

"Madame, your wife," said Cecil, with the grave politeness of an old man, "has done me the honor to take me into her confidence. She tells me that you have won a great deal of money; that you could put it to good use at home, and so save yourselves much drudgery and debt, and all that sort of trouble. You are quite right if you say it is no concern of mine. It is not. But really, you know there is a great deal of sense in what she wants, and you have apparently already won a large sum."

The Frenchman was visibly surprised at this approach. He paused for a second or two in some doubt, and even awe, for the disinherited one carried the mark of a personage of consideration and of one whose position is secure. Then he gave a short, unmirthful laugh.

"You are most kind, sir," he said with mock politeness and with an impatient shrug. "But madame, my wife, has not done well to interest a stranger in this affair, which, as you say, concerns you not."

He turned to the table again with a defiant swagger of independence and placed two rolls of money upon the cloth, casting at the same moment a childish look of displeasure at his wife. "You see," said the Plunger, with a deprecatory turning out of his hands. But there was so much grief on the girl's face that he turned again to the gambler and touched his arm. He could not tell why he was so interested in these two. He had witnessed many such scenes before, and they had not affected him in any way except to make him move out of hearing. But the same dumb numbness in his head, which made so many things seem possible that should have been terrible even to think upon, made him stubborn and unreasonable over this. He felt intuitively - it could not be said that he thought - that the woman was right and the man wrong, and so he grasped him again by the arm, and said sharply this time:

"Come away! Do you hear? You are acting foolishly."

But even as he spoke the red won, and the Frenchman with a boyish gurgle of pleasure raked in his winnings with his two hands, and then turned with a happy, triumphant laugh to his wife. It is not easy to convince a man that he is making a fool of himself when he is winning some hundred francs every two minutes. His silent arguments to the contrary are difficult to answer. But the Plunger did not regard this in the least.

"Do you hear me?" he said in the same stubborn tone and with much the same manner with which he would have spoken to a groom. "Come away."

Again the Frenchman tossed off his hand, this time with an execration, and again he placed the rolls of gold coin on the red; and again the red won.

"My God!" cried the girl, running her fingers over the rolls on the table, "he has won half of the 20,000 francs. Oh, sir, stop him, stop him!" she cried. "Take him away."

"Do you hear me!" cried the Plunger, excited to a degree of utter self-forgetfulness, and carried beyond himself; "you've got to come with me."

"Take away your hand," whispered the young Frenchman, fiercely. "See, I shall win it all; in one grand *coup* I shall win it all. I shall win five years' pay in one moment."

He swept all of the money forward on the red and threw himself over the table to see the wheel.

"Wait, confound you!" whispered the Plunger, excitedly. "If you will risk it, risk it with some reason. You can't play all that money; they won't take it. Six thousand francs is the limit, unless," he ran on quickly, "you divide the 12,000 francs among the three of us. You understand, 6,000 francs is all that any one person can play; but if you give 4,000 to me, and 4,000 to your wife, and keep 4,000 yourself, we can each chance it. You can back the red if you like, your wife shall put her money on the numbers coming up below eighteen, and I will back the odd. In that way you stand to win 24,000 francs if our combination wins, and you lose less than if you simply back the color. Do you understand?"

"No!" cried the Frenchman, reaching for the piles of money which the Plunger had divided rapidly into three parts, "on the red; all on the red!"

"Good heavens, man!" cried the Plunger, bitterly. "I may not know much, but you should allow me to understand this dirty business." He caught the Frenchman by the wrists, and the young man, more impressed with the strange look in the boy's face than by his physical force, stood still, while the ball rolled and rolled, and clicked merrily, and stopped, and balanced, and then settled into the "seven."

"Red, odd, and below," the croupier droned mechanically.

"Ah! you see; what did I tell you?" said the Plunger, with sudden calmness. "You have won more than your 20,000 francs; you are proprietors - I congratulate you!"

"Ah, my God!" cried the Frenchman, in a frenzy of delight, "I will double it."

He reached toward the fresh piles of coin as if he meant to sweep them back again, but the Plunger put himself in his way and with a quick movement caught up the rolls of money and dropped them into the skirt of the woman, which she raised like an apron to receive her treasure.

"Now," said young Harringford, determinedly, "you come with me." The Frenchman tried to argue and resist, but the Plunger pushed him on with the silent stubbornness of a drunken man. He handed the woman into a carriage at the door, shoved her husband in beside her, and while the man drove to the address she gave him, he told the Frenchman, with an air of a chief of police, that he must leave Monte Carlo at once, that very night.

"Do you suppose I don't know?" he said. "Do you fancy I speak without knowledge? I've seen them come here rich and go away paupers. But you shall not; you shall keep what you have and spite them." He sent the woman up to her room to pack while he expostulated with and browbeat the excited bridegroom in the carriage. When she returned with the bag packed, and so heavy with the gold that the servants could hardly lift it up beside the driver, he ordered the coachman to go down the hill to the station.

"The train for Paris leaves at midnight," he said, "and you will be there by morning. Then you must close your bargain with this old Carbut, and never return here again."

The Frenchman had turned during the ride from an angry, indignant prisoner to a joyful madman, and was now tearfully and effusively humble in his petitions for pardon and in his thanks. Their benefactor, as they were pleased to call him, hurried them into the waiting train and ran to purchase their tickets for them.

"Now," he said, as the guard locked the door of the compartment, "you are alone, and no one can get in, and you cannot get out. Go back to your home, to your new home, and never come to this wretched place again. Promise me - you understand? - never again!"

They promised with effusive reiteration. They embraced each other like children, and the man, pulling off his hat, called upon the good Lord to thank the gentleman.

"You will be in Paris, will you not?" said the woman, in an ecstasy of pleasure, "and you will come to see us in our own shop, will you not? Ah! we should be so greatly honored, sir, if you would visit us; if you would come to the home you have given us. You have helped us so greatly, sir," she said; "and may Heaven bless you!"

She caught up his gloved hand as it rested on the door and kissed it until he snatched it away in great embarrassment and flushing like a girl. Her husband drew her toward him, and the young bride sat at his side with her face close to his and wept tears of pleasure and of excitement.

"Ah, look, sir!" said the young man, joyfully; "look how happy you have made us. You have made us happy for the rest of our lives."

The train moved out with a quick, heavy rush, and the car-wheels took up the young stranger's last words and seemed to say, "You have made us happy - made us happy for the rest of our lives."

It had all come about so rapidly that the Plunger had

had no time to consider or to weigh his motives, and all that seemed real to him now, as he stood alone on the platform of the dark, deserted station, were the words of the man echoing and re-echoing like the refrain of the song. And then there came to him suddenly, and with all the force of a gambler's super-stition, the thought that the words were the same as those which his father had used in his letter, "you can make us happy for the rest of our lives."

"Ah," he said, with a quick gasp of doubt, "if I could! If I made those poor fools happy, mayn't I live to be something to him, and to her? O God!" he cried, but so gently that one at his elbow could not have heard him, "if I could, if I could!"

He tossed up his hands, and drew them down again and clenched them in front of him, and raised his tired, hot eyes to the calm purple sky with its millions of moving stars. "Help me!" he whispered fiercely, "help me." And as he lowered his head the queer numb feeling seemed to go, and a calm came over his nerves and left him in peace. He did not know what it might be, nor did he dare to question the change which had come to him, but turned and slowly mounted the hill, with the awe and fear still upon him of one who had passed beyond himself for one brief moment into another world. When he reached his room he found his servant bending with an anxious face over a letter which he tore up guiltily as his master entered. "You were writing to my father," said Cecil, gently, "were you not? Well, you need not finish your letter; we are going home.

"I am going away from this place, Walters," he said as he pulled off his coat and threw himself heavily on the bed. "I will take the first train that leaves here, and I will sleep a little while you put up my things. The first train, you understand - within an hour, if it leaves that soon." His head sank back on the pillows heavily, as though he had come in from a long, weary walk, and his eyes closed and his arms fell easily at his side. The servant stood frightened and yet happy, with the tears running down his cheeks, for he loved his master dearly.

"We are going home, Walters," the Plunger whispered drowsily. "We are going home; home to England and Harringford and the governor - and we are going to be happy for all the rest of our lives." He paused a moment, and Walters bent forward over the bed and held his breath to listen.

"For he came to me," murmured the boy, as though he was speaking in his sleep, "when I was yet a great way off - while I was yet a great way off, and ran to meet me -"

His voice sank until it died away into silence, and a few hours later, when Walters came to wake him, he found his master sleeping like a child and smiling in his sleep.

THE CYNICAL MISS CATHERWAIGHT

Miss Catherwaight's collection of orders and decorations and medals was her chief offence in the eyes of those of her dear friends who thought her clever but cynical.

All of them were willing to admit that she was clever, but some of them said she was clever only to be unkind.

Young Van Bibber had said that if Miss Catherwaight did not like dances and days and teas, she had only to stop going to them instead of making unpleasant remarks about those who did. So many people repeated this that young Van Bibber believed finally that he had said something good, and was somewhat pleased in consequence, as he was not much given to that sort of thing.

Mrs. Catherwaight, while she was alive, lived solely for society, and, so some people said, not only lived but died for it. She certainly did go about a great deal, and she used to carry her husband away from his library every night of every season and left him standing in the doorways of drawing-rooms, outwardly courteous and distinguished looking, but inwardly somnolent and unhappy. She was a born and trained social leader, and her daughter's coming out was to have been the greatest effort of her life. She regarded it as an event in the dear child's lifetime second only in importance to her birth; equally important with her probable marriage and of much more poignant interest than her possible death. But the great effort proved too much for the mother, and she died, fondly remembered by her peers and tenderly referred to by a great many people who could not even show a card for her Thursdays. Her husband and her daughter were not going out, of necessity, for more than a year after her death, and then felt no inclination to begin over again, but lived very much together and showed themselves only occasionally.

They entertained, though, a great deal, in the way of dinners, and an invitation to one of these dinners soon became a diploma for intellectual as well as social qualifications of a very high order.

One was always sure of meeting some one of consideration there, which was pleasant in itself, and also rendered it easy to let one's friends know where one had been dining. It sounded so flat to boast abruptly, "I dined at the Catherwaights' last night"; while it seemed only natural to remark, "That reminds me of a story that novelist, what's his name, told at Mr. Catherwaight's," or "That English chap, who's been in Africa, was at the Catherwaights' the other night, and told me -"

After one of these dinners people always asked to be allowed to look over Miss Catherwaight's collection, of which almost everybody had heard. It consisted of over a hundred medals and decorations which Miss Catherwaight had purchased while on the long tours she made with her father in all parts of the world. Each of them had been given as a reward for some public service, as a recognition of some virtue of the highest order - for personal bravery, for statesmanship, for great genius in the arts; and each had been pawned by the recipient or sold outright. Miss Catherwaight referred to them as her collection of dishonored honors, and called them variously her Orders of the Knights of the Almighty Dollar, pledges to patriotism and the pawnshops, and honors at second-hand.

It was her particular fad to get as many of these together as she could and to know the story of each. The less creditable the story, the more highly she valued the medal. People might think it was not a pretty hobby for a young girl, but they could not help smiling at the stories and at the scorn with which she told them.

"These," she would say, "are crosses of the Legion of Honor; they are of the lowest degree, that of chevalier. I keep them in this cigar box to show how cheaply I got them and how cheaply I hold them. I think you can get them here in New York for ten dollars; they cost more than that - about a hundred francs - in Paris. At second-hand, of course. The French government can imprison you, you know, for ten years, if you wear one without the right to do so, but they have no punishment for those who choose to part with them for a mess of pottage.

"All these," she would run on, "are English war medals. See, on this one is 'Alma,' 'Balaclava,' and 'Sebastopol.' He was quite a veteran, was he not? Well, he sold this to a dealer on Wardour Street, London, for five and six. You can get any number of them on the Bowery for their weight in silver. I tried very hard to get a Victoria Cross when I was in England, and I only succeeded in getting this one after a great deal of trouble. They value the cross so highly, you know, that it is the only other decoration in the case which holds the Order of the Garter in the Jewel Room at the Tower. It is made of copper, so that its intrinsic value won't have any weight with the man who gets it, but I bought this nevertheless for five pounds. The soldier to whom it belonged had loaded and fired a cannon all alone when the rest of the men about the battery had run away. He was captured by the enemy, but retaken immediately afterward by re-enforcements from his own side, and the general in command recommended him to the Queen for decoration. He sold his cross to the proprietor of a curiosity shop and drank himself to death. I felt rather meanly about keeping it and hunted up his widow to return it to her, but she said I could have it for a consideration.

"This gold medal was given, as you see, to 'Hiram J. Stillman, of the sloop *Annie Barker*, for saving the crew of the steamship *Olivia*, June 18, 1888,' by the President of the United States and both houses of Congress. I found it on Baxter Street in a pawnshop. The gallant Hiram J. had pawned it for sixteen dollars and never came back to claim it."

"But, Miss Catherwaight," some optimist would object, "these men undoubtedly did do something brave and noble once. You can't get back of that; and they didn't do it for a medal, either, but because it was their duty. And so the medal meant nothing to them: their conscience told them they had done the right thing; they didn't need a stamped coin to remind them of it, or of their wounds, either, perhaps."

"Quite right; that's quite true," Miss Catherwaight would say. "But how about this? Look at this gold medal with the diamonds: 'Presented to Colonel James F. Placer by the men of his regiment, in camp before Richmond.' Every soldier in the regiment gave something toward that, and yet the brave gentleman put it up at a game of poker one night, and the officer who won it sold it to the man who gave it to me. Can you defend that?"

Miss Catherwaight was well known to the proprietors of the pawnshops and loan offices on the Bowery and Park Row. They learned to look for her once a month, and saved what medals they received for her and tried to learn their stories from the people who pawned them, or else invented some story which they hoped would answer just as well.

Though her brougham produced a sensation in the unfashionable streets into which she directed it, she was never annoyed. Her maid went with her into the shops, and one of the grooms always stood at the door within call, to the intense delight of the neighborhood. And one day she found what, from her point of view, was a perfect gem. It was a poor, cheap-looking, tarnished silver medal, a half-dollar once, undoubtedly, beaten out roughly into the shape of a heart and engraved in script by the jeweller of some country town. On one side were two clasped hands with a wreath around them, and on the reverse was this inscription: "From Henry Burgoyne to his beloved friend Lewis L. Lockwood"; and below, "Through prosperity and adversity." That was all. And here it was among razors and pistols and family Bibles in a pawnbroker's window. What a story there was in that! These two boy friends, and their boyish friendship that was to withstand adversity and prosperity, and all that remained of it was this inscription to its memory like the wording on a tomb!

"He couldn't have got so much on it any way," said the pawnbroker, entering into her humor. "I didn't lend him more'n a quarter of a dollar at the most."

Miss Catherwaight stood wondering if the Lewis L. Lockwood could be Lewis Lockwood, the lawyer one read so much about. Then she remembered his middle name was Lyman, and said quickly, "I'll take it, please."

She stepped into the carriage, and told the man to go find a directory and look for Lewis Lyman Lockwood. The groom returned in a few minutes and said there was such a name down in the book as a lawyer, and that his office was such a number on Broadway; it must be near Liberty. "Go there," said Miss Catherwaight.

Her determination was made so quickly that they had stopped in front of a huge pile of offices, sandwiched in, one above the other, until they towered mountains high, before she had quite settled in her mind what she wanted to know, or had appreciated how strange her errand might appear. Mr. Lockwood was out, one of the young men in the outer office said, but the junior partner, Mr. Latimer, was in and would see her. She had only time to remember that the junior partner was a dancing acquaintance of hers, before young Mr. Latimer stood before her smiling, and with her card in his hand.

"Mr. Lockwood is out just at present, Miss Catherwaight," he said, "but he will be back in a moment. Won't you come into the other room and wait? I'm sure he won't be away over five minutes. Or is it something I could do?"

She saw that he was surprised to see her, and a little ill at ease as to just how to take her visit. He tried to make it appear that he considered it the most natural thing in the world, but he overdid it, and she saw that her presence was something quite out of the common. This did not tend to set her any more at her ease. She already regretted the step she had taken. What if it should prove to be the same Lockwood, she thought, and what would they think of her?

"Perhaps you will do better than Mr. Lockwood," she said, as she followed him into the inner office. "I fear I have come upon a very foolish errand, and one that has nothing at all to do with the law."

"Not a breach of promise suit, then?" said young Latimer, with a smile. "Perhaps it is only an innocent subscription to a most worthy charity. I was afraid at first," he went on lightly, "that it was legal redress you wanted, and I was hoping that the way I led the Courdert's cotillion had made you think I could conduct you through the mazes of the law as well."

"No," returned Miss Catherwaight, with a nervous laugh; "it has to do with my unfortunate collection. This is what brought me here," she said, holding out the silver medal. "I came across it just now in the Bowery. The name was the same, and I thought it just possible Mr. Lockwood would like to have it; or, to tell you the truth, that he might tell me what had become of the Henry Burgoyne who gave it to him."

Young Latimer had the medal in his hand before she had finished speaking, and was examining it carefully. He looked up with just a touch of color in his cheeks and straightened himself visibly.

"Please don't be offended," said the fair collector. "I know what you think. You've heard of my stupid collection, and I know you think I meant to add this to it. But, indeed, now that I have had time to think - you see I came here immediately from the pawnshop, and I was so interested, like all collectors, you know, that I didn't stop to consider. That's the worst of a hobby; it carries one rough-shod over other people's feelings, and runs away with one. I beg of you, if you do know anything about the coin, just to keep it and don't tell me, and I assure you what little I know I will keep quite to myself."

Young Latimer bowed, and stood looking at her curiously, with the medal in his hand.

"I hardly know what to say," he began slowly. "It really has a story. You say you found this on the Bowery, in a pawnshop. Indeed! Well, of course, you know Mr. Lockwood could not have left it there."

Miss Catherwaight shook her head vehemently and smiled in deprecation.

"This medal was in his safe when he lived on Thirty-fifth Street at the time he was robbed, and the burglars took this with the rest of the silver and pawned it, I suppose. Mr. Lockwood would have given more for it than any one else could have afforded to pay." He paused a moment, and then continued more rapidly: "Henry Burgoyne is Judge Burgoyne. Ah! you didn't guess that? Yes, Mr. Lockwood and he were friends when they were boys. They went to school in Westchester County. They were Damon and Pythias and that sort of thing. They roomed together at the State college and started to practise law in Tuckahoe as a firm, but they made nothing of it, and came on to New York and began reading law again with Fuller & Mowbray. It was while they were at school that they had these medals made. There was a mate to this, you know; Judge Burgoyne had it. Well, they continued to live and work together. They were both orphans and dependent on themselves. I suppose that was one of the strongest bonds between them; and they knew no one in New York, and always spent their spare time together. They were pretty poor, I fancy, from all Mr. Lockwood has told me, but they were very ambitious. They were - I'm telling you this, you understand, because it concerns you somewhat: well, more or less. They were great sportsmen, and whenever they could get away from the law office they would go off shooting. I think they were fonder of each other than brothers even. I've heard Mr. Lockwood tell of the days they lay in the rushes along the Chesapeake Bay waiting for duck. He has said often that they were the happiest hours of his life. That was their greatest pleasure, going off together after duck or snipe along the Maryland waters. Well, they grew rich and began to know people; and then they met a girl. It seems they both thought a great deal of her, as half the New York men did, I am told; and she was the reigning belle and toast, and had other admirers, and neither met with that favor she showed - well, the man she married, for instance. But for a while each thought, for some reason or other, that he was especially favored. I don't know anything about it. Mr. Lockwood never spoke of it to me. But they both fell very deeply in love with her, and each thought the other disloyal, and so they quarrelled; and - and then, though the woman married, the two men kept apart. It was the one great passion of their lives, and both were proud, and each thought the other in the wrong, and so they have kept apart ever since. And - well, I believe that is all."

Miss Catherwaight had listened in silence and with one little gloved hand tightly clasping the other.

"Indeed, Mr. Latimer, indeed," she began, tremulously, "I am terribly ashamed of myself. I seemed to have rushed in where angels fear to tread. I wouldn't meet Mr. Lockwood *now* for worlds. Of course I might have known there was a woman in the case, it adds so much to the story. But I suppose I must give up my medal. I never could tell that story, could I?"

"No," said young Latimer, dryly; "I wouldn't if I were you."

Something in his tone, and something in the fact that he seemed to avoid her eyes, made her drop the lighter vein in which she had been speaking, and rise to go. There was much that he had not told her, she suspected, and when she bade him good-by it was with a reserve which she had not shown at any other time during their interview.

"I wonder who that woman was?" she murmured, as young Latimer turned from the brougham door and said "Home," to the groom. She thought about it a great deal that afternoon; at times she repented that she had given up the medal, and at times she blushed that she should have been carried in her zeal into such an unwarranted intimacy with another's story.

She determined finally to ask her father about it. He would be sure to know, she thought, as he and Mr. Lockwood were contemporaries. Then she decided finally not to say anything about it at all, for Mr. Catherwaight did not approve of the collection of dishonored honors as it was, and she had no desire to prejudice him still further by a recital of her afternoon's adventure, of which she had no doubt but he would also disapprove. So she was more than usually silent during the dinner, which was a tete-a-tete family dinner that night, and she allowed her father to doze after it in the library in his great chair without disturbing him with either questions or confessions.

They had been sitting there some time, he with his hands folded on the evening paper and with his eyes closed, when the servant brought in a card and offered it to Mr. Catherwaight. Mr. Catherwaight fumbled over his glasses, and read the name on the card aloud: "'Mr. Lewis L. Lockwood.' Dear me!" he said; "what can Mr. Lockwood be calling upon me about?"

Miss Catherwaight sat upright, and reached out for the card with a nervous, gasping little laugh.

"Oh, I think it must be for me," she said; "I'm quite sure it is intended for me. I was at his office to-day, you see, to return him some keepsake of his that I found in an old curiosity shop. Something with his name on it that had been stolen from him and pawned. It was just a trifle. You needn't go down, dear; I'll see him. It was I he asked for, I'm sure; was it not, Morris?"

Morris was not quite sure; being such an old gentleman, he thought it must be for Mr. Catherwaight he'd come.

Mr. Catherwaight was not greatly interested. He did not like to disturb his after-dinner nap, and he settled back in his chair again and refolded his hands.

"I hardly thought he could have come to see me," he murmured, drowsily; "though I used to see enough and more than enough of Lewis Lockwood once, my dear," he added with a smile, as he opened his eyes and nodded before he shut them again. "That was before your mother and I were engaged, and people did say that young Lockwood's chances at that time were as good as mine. But they weren't, it seems. He was very attentive, though; *very* attentive."

Miss Catherwaight stood startled and motionless at the door from which she had turned.

"Attentive - to whom?" she asked quickly, and in a very low voice. "To my mother?"

Mr. Catherwaight did not deign to open his eyes this time, but moved his head uneasily as if he wished to be let alone.

"To your mother, of course, my child," he answered; "of whom else was I speaking?"

Miss Catherwaight went down the stairs to the drawing-room slowly, and paused half-way to allow this new suggestion to settle in her mind. There was something distasteful to her, something that seemed not altogether unblamable, in a woman's having two men quarrel about her, neither of whom was the woman's husband. And yet this girl of whom Latimer had spoken must be her mother, and she, of course, could do no wrong. It was very disquieting, and she went on down the rest of the way with one hand resting heavily on the railing and with the other pressed against her cheeks. She was greatly troubled. It now seemed to her very sad indeed that these two one-time friends should live in the same city and meet, as they must meet, and not recognize each other. She argued that her mother must have been very young when it happened, or she would have brought two such men together again. Her mother could not have known, she told herself; she was not to blame. For she felt sure that had she herself known of such an accident she would have done something, said something, to make it right. And she was not half the woman her mother had been, she was sure of that.

There was something very likable in the old gentleman who came forward to greet her as she entered the drawing-room; something courtly and of the old school, of which she was so tired of hearing, but of which she wished she could have seen more in the men she met. Young Mr. Latimer had accompanied his guardian, exactly why she did not see, but she recognized his presence slightly. He seemed quite content to remain in the background. Mr. Lockwood, as she had expected, explained that he had called to thank her for the return of the medal. He had it in his hand as he spoke, and touched it gently with the tips of his fingers as though caressing it.

"I knew your father very well," said the lawyer, "and I at one time had the honor of being one of your mother's younger friends. That was before she was married, many years ago." He stopped and regarded the girl gravely and with a touch of tenderness. "You will pardon an old man, old enough to be your father, if he says," he went on, "that you are greatly like your

mother, my dear young lady - greatly like. Your
mother was very kind to me, and I fear I abused her
kindness; abused it by misunderstanding it. There was
a great deal of misunderstanding; and I was proud, and
my friend was proud, and so the misunderstanding
continued, until now it has become irretrievable."

He had forgotten her presence apparently, and was
speaking more to himself than to her as he stood
looking down at the medal in his hand.

"You were very thoughtful to give me this," he
continued; "it was very good of you. I don't know why
I should keep it though, now, although I was distressed
enough when I lost it. But now it is only a reminder of
a time that is past and put away, but which was very,
very dear to me. Perhaps I should tell you that I had a
misunderstanding with the friend who gave it to me,
and since then we have never met; have ceased to
know each other. But I have always followed his life as
a judge and as a lawyer, and respected him for his own
sake as a man. I cannot tell - I do not know how he
feels toward me."

The old lawyer turned the medal over in his hand and
stood looking down at it wistfully.

The cynical Miss Catherwaight could not stand it any
longer.

"Mr. Lockwood," she said, impulsively, "Mr. Latimer
has told me why you and your friend separated, and I
cannot bear to think that it was she - my mother -
should have been the cause. She could not have understood; she must have been innocent of any knowledge
of the trouble she had brought to men who were such

good friends of hers and to each other. It seems to me as though my finding that coin is more than a coincidence. I somehow think that the daughter is to help undo the harm that her mother has caused - unwittingly caused. Keep the medal and don't give it back to me, for I am sure your friend has kept his, and I am sure he is still your friend at heart. Don't think I am speaking hastily or that I am thoughtless in what I am saying, but it seems to me as if friends - good, true friends - were so few that one cannot let them go without a word to bring them back. But though I am only a girl, and a very light and unfeeling girl, some people think, I feel this very much, and I do wish I could bring your old friend back to you again as I brought back his pledge."

"It has been many years since Henry Burgoyne and I have met," said the old man, slowly, "and it would be quite absurd to think that he still holds any trace of that foolish, boyish feeling of loyalty that we once had for each other. Yet I will keep this, if you will let me, and I thank you, my dear young lady, for what you have said. I thank you from the bottom of my heart. You are as good and as kind as your mother was, and - I can say nothing, believe me, in higher praise."

He rose slowly and made a movement as if to leave the room, and then, as if the excitement of this sudden return into the past could not be shaken off so readily, he started forward with a move of sudden determination.

"I think," he said, "I will go to Henry Burgoyne's house at once, to-night. I will act on what you have suggested. I will see if this has or has not been one long, unprofitable mistake. If my visit should be fruitless, I will send you this coin to add to your collection of dishonored honors, but if it should result as I hope it may, it will be your doing, Miss Catherwaight, and two old men will have much to thank you for. Good-night," he said as he bowed above her hand, "and - God bless you!"

Miss Catherwaight flushed slightly at what he had said, and sat looking down at the floor for a moment after the door had closed behind him.

Young Mr. Latimer moved uneasily in his chair. The routine of the office had been strangely disturbed that day, and he now failed to recognize in the girl before him with reddened cheeks and trembling eyelashes the cold, self-possessed young woman of society whom he had formerly known.

"You have done very well, if you will let me say so," he began, gently. "I hope you are right in what you said, and that Mr. Lockwood will not meet with a rebuff or an ungracious answer. Why," he went on quickly, "I have seen him take out his gun now every spring and every fall for the last ten years and clean and polish it and tell what great shots he and Henry, as he calls him, used to be. And then he would say he would take a holiday and get off for a little shooting. But he never went. He would put the gun back into its case again and mope in his library for days afterward. You see, he never married, and though he adopted me, in a manner, and is fond of me in a certain way, no one ever took the place in his heart his old friend had held."

"You will let me know, will you not, at once, - to-night, even, - whether he succeeds or not?" said the cynical Miss Catherwaight. "You can understand why I am so deeply interested. I see now why you said I would not tell the story of that medal. But, after all, it may be the prettiest story, the only pretty story I have to tell."

Mr. Lockwood had not returned, the man said, when young Latimer reached the home the lawyer had made for them both. He did not know what to argue from this, but determined to sit up and wait, and so sat smoking before the fire and listening with his sense of hearing on a strain for the first movement at the door.

He had not long to wait. The front door shut with a clash, and he heard Mr. Lockwood crossing the hall quickly to the library, in which he waited. Then the inner door was swung back, and Mr. Lockwood came in with his head high and his eyes smiling brightly.

There was something in his step that had not been there before, something light and vigorous, and he looked ten years younger. He crossed the room to his writing-table without speaking and began tossing the papers about on his desk. Then he closed the rolling-top lid with a snap and looked up smiling.

"I shall have to ask you to look after things at the office for a little while," he said. "Judge Burgoyne and I are going to Maryland for a few weeks' shooting."

VAN BIBBER AND THE SWAN-BOATS

It was very hot in the Park, and young Van Bibber, who has a good heart and a great deal more money than good-hearted people generally get, was cross and somnolent. He had told his groom to bring a horse he wanted to try to the Fifty-ninth Street entrance at ten o'clock, and the groom had not appeared. Hence Van Bibber's crossness.

He waited as long as his dignity would allow, and then turned off into a by-lane end dropped on a bench and looked gloomily at the Lohengrin swans with the paddle-wheel attachment that circle around the lake. They struck him as the most idiotic inventions he had ever seen, and he pitied, with the pity of a man who contemplates crossing the ocean to be measured for his fall clothes, the people who could find delight in having some one paddle them around an artificial lake.

Two little girls from the East Side, with a lunch basket, and an older girl with her hair down her back, sat down on a bench beside him and gazed at the swans.

The place was becoming too popular, and Van Bibber decided to move on. But the bench on which he sat was in the shade, and the asphalt walk leading to the street was in the sun, and his cigarette was soothing, so he ignored the near presence of the three little girls, and remained where he was.

"I s'pose," said one of the two little girls, in a high, public school voice, "there's lots to see from those swan-boats that youse can't see from the banks."

"Oh, lots," assented the girl with long hair.

"If you walked all round the lake, clear all the way round, you could see all there is to see," said the third, "except what there's in the middle where the island is."

"I guess it's mighty wild on that island," suggested the youngest.

"Eddie Case he took a trip around the lake on a swan-boat the other day. He said that it was grand. He said youse could see fishes and ducks, and that it looked just as if there were snakes and things on the island."

"What sort of things?" asked the other one, in a hushed voice.

"Well, wild things," explained the elder, vaguely; "bears and animals like that, that grow in wild places."

Van Bibber lit a fresh cigarette, and settled himself comfortably and unreservedly to listen.

"My, but I'd like to take a trip just once," said the youngest, under her breath. Then she clasped her fingers together and looked up anxiously at the elder girl, who glanced at her with severe reproach.

"Why, Mame!" she said; "ain't you ashamed! Ain't you having a good time 'nuff without wishing for everything you set your eyes on?"

Van Bibber wondered at this - why humans should want to ride around on the swans in the first place, and why, if they had such a wild desire, they should not gratify it.

"Why, it costs more'n it costs to come all the way up town in an open car," added the elder girl, as if in answer to his unspoken question.

The younger girl sighed at this, and nodded her head in submission, but blinked longingly at the big swans and the parti-colored awning and the red seats.

"I beg your pardon," said Van Bibber, addressing himself uneasily to the eldest girl with long hair, "but if the little girl would like to go around in one of those things, and - and hasn't brought the change with her, you know, I'm sure I should be very glad if she'd allow me to send her around."

"Oh! will you?" exclaimed the little girl, with a jump, and so sharply and in such a shrill voice that Van Bibber shuddered. But the elder girl objected.

"I'm afraid maw wouldn't like our taking money from any one we didn't know," she said with dignity; "but if you're going anyway and want company -"

"Oh! my, no," said Van Bibber, hurriedly. He tried to picture himself riding around the lake behind a tin swan with three little girls from the East Side, and a lunch basket.

"Then," said the head of the trio, "we can't go."

There was such a look of uncomplaining acceptance of this verdict on the part of the two little girls, that Van Bibber felt uncomfortable. He looked to the right and to the left, and then said desperately, "Well, come along." The young man in a blue flannel shirt, who did the paddling, smiled at Van Bibber's riding-breeches, which were so very loose at one end and so very tight at the other, and at his gloves and crop. But Van Bibber pretended not to care. The three little girls placed the awful lunch basket on the front seat and sat on the middle one, and Van Bibber cowered in the back. They were hushed in silent ecstasy when it started, and gave little gasps of pleasure when it careened slightly in turning. It was shady under the awning, and the motion was pleasant enough, but Van Bibber was so afraid some one would see him that he failed to enjoy it.

But as soon as they passed into the narrow straits and were shut in by the bushes and were out of sight of the people, he relaxed, and began to play the host. He pointed out the fishes among the rocks at the edges of the pool, and the sparrows and robins bathing and ruffling their feathers in the shallow water, and agreed with them about the possibility of bears, and even tigers, in the wild part of the island, although the glimpse of the gray helmet of a Park policeman made such a supposition doubtful.

And it really seemed as though they were enjoying it more than he ever enjoyed a trip up the Sound on a yacht or across the ocean on a record-breaking steamship. It seemed long enough before they got back to Van Bibber, but his guests were evidently but barely satisfied. Still, all the goodness in his nature would not allow him to go through that ordeal again.

He stepped out of the boat eagerly and helped out the girl with long hair as though she had been a princess and tipped the rude young man who had laughed at him, but who was perspiring now with the work he had done; and then as he turned to leave the dock he came face to face with A Girl He Knew and Her brother.

Her brother said, "How're you, Van Bibber? Been taking a trip around the world in eighty minutes?" And added in a low voice, "Introduce me to your young lady friends from Hester Street."

"Ah, how're you - quite a surprise!" gasped Van Bibber, while his late guests stared admiringly at the pretty young lady in the riding-habit, and utterly refused to move on. "Been taking ride on the lake," stammered Van Bibber; "most exhilarating. Young friends of mine - these young ladies never rode on lake, so I took 'em. Did you see me?"

"Oh, yes, we saw you," said Her brother, dryly, while she only smiled at him, but so kindly and with such perfect understanding that Van Bibber grew red with pleasure and bought three long strings of tickets for the swans at some absurd discount, and gave each little girl a string.

"There," said Her brother to the little ladies from Hester Street, "now you can take trips for a week without stopping. Don't try to smuggle in any laces, and don't forget to fee the smoking-room steward."

The Girl He Knew said they were walking over to the stables, and that he had better go get his other horse and join her, which was to be his reward for taking care of the young ladies. And the three little girls proceeded to use up the yards of tickets so industriously that they were sunburned when they reached the tenement, and went to bed dreaming of a big white swan, and a beautiful young gentleman in patent-leather riding-boots and baggy breeches.

VAN BIBBER'S BURGLAR

There had been a dance up town, but as Van Bibber could not find Her there, he accepted young Travers's suggestion to go over to Jersey City and see a "go" between "Dutchy" Mack and a colored person professionally known as the Black Diamond. They covered up all signs of their evening dress with their great-coats, and filled their pockets with cigars, for the smoke which surrounds a "go" is trying to sensitive nostrils, and they also fastened their watches to both key-chains. Alf Alpin, who was acting as master of ceremonies, was greatly pleased and flattered at their coming, and boisterously insisted on their sitting on the platform. The fact was generally circulated among the spectators that the "two gents in high hats" had come in a carriage, and this and their patent-leather boots made them objects of keen interest. It was even whispered that they were the "parties" who were putting up the money to back the Black Diamond against the "Hester Street Jackson." This in itself entitled them to respect. Van Bibber was asked to hold the watch, but he wisely declined the honor, which was given to Andy Spielman, the sporting reporter of the *Track and Ring*, whose watch-case was covered with diamonds, and was just the sort of a watch a timekeeper should hold.

It was two o'clock before "Dutchy" Mack's backer

threw the sponge into the air, and three before they reached the city. They had another reporter in the cab with them besides the gentleman who had bravely held the watch in the face of several offers to "do for" him; and as Van Bibber was ravenously hungry, and as he doubted that he could get anything at that hour at the club, they accepted Spielman's invitation and went for a porterhouse steak and onions at the Owl's Nest, Gus McGowan's all-night restaurant on Third Avenue.

It was a very dingy, dirty place, but it was as warm as the engine-room of a steamboat, and the steak was perfectly done and tender. It was too late to go to bed, so they sat around the table, with their chairs tipped back and their knees against its edge. The two club men had thrown off their great-coats, and their wide shirt fronts and silk facings shone grandly in the smoky light of the oil lamps and the red glow from the grill in the corner. They talked about the life the reporters led, and the Philistines asked foolish questions, which the gentleman of the press answered without showing them how foolish they were.

"And I suppose you have all sorts of curious adventures," said Van Bibber, tentatively.

"Well, no, not what I would call adventures," said one of the reporters. "I have never seen anything that could not be explained or attributed directly to some known cause, such as crime or poverty or drink. You may think at first that you have stumbled on something strange and romantic, but it comes to nothing. You would suppose that in a great city like this one would come across something that could not be explained away something mysterious or out of the common, like Stevenson's Suicide Club. But I have not found it so.

Dickens once told James Payn that the most curious thing he ever saw In his rambles around London was a ragged man who stood crouching under the window of a great house where the owner was giving a ball. While the man hid beneath a window on the ground floor, a woman wonderfully dressed and very beautiful raised the sash from the inside and dropped her bouquet down into the man's hand, and he nodded and stuck it under his coat and ran off with it.

"I call that, now, a really curious thing to see. But I have never come across anything like it, and I have been in every part of this big city, and at every hour of the night and morning, and I am not lacking in imagination either, but no captured maidens have ever beckoned to me from barred windows nor 'white hands waved from a passing hansom.' Balzac and De Musset and Stevenson suggest that they have had such adventures, but they never come to me. It is all commonplace and vulgar, and always ends in a police court or with a 'found drowned' in the North River."

McGowan, who had fallen into a doze behind the bar, woke suddenly and shivered and rubbed his shirt-sleeves briskly. A woman knocked at the side door and begged for a drink "for the love of heaven," and the man who tended the grill told her to be off. They could hear her feeling her way against the wall and cursing as she staggered out of the alley. Three men came in with a hack driver and wanted everybody to drink with them, and became insolent when the gentlemen declined, and were in consequence hustled out one at a time by McGowan, who went to sleep again immediately, with his head resting among the cigar boxes and pyramids of glasses at the back of the bar, and snored.

"You see," said the reporter, "it is all like this. Night in a great city is not picturesque and it is not theatrical. It is sodden, sometimes brutal, exciting enough until you get used to it, but it runs in a groove. It is dramatic, but the plot is old and the motives and characters always the same."

The rumble of heavy market wagons and the rattle of milk carts told them that it was morning, and as they opened the door the cold fresh air swept into the place and made them wrap their collars around their throats and stamp their feet. The morning wind swept down the cross-street from the East River and the lights of the street lamps and of the saloon looked old and tawdry. Travers and the reporter went off to a Turkish bath, and the gentleman who held the watch, and who had been asleep for the last hour, dropped into a nighthawk and told the man to drive home. It was almost clear now and very cold, and Van Bibber determined to walk. He had the strange feeling one gets when one stays up until the sun rises, of having lost a day somewhere, and the dance he had attended a few hours before seemed to have come off long ago, and the fight in Jersey City was far back in the past.

The houses along the cross-street through which he walked were as dead as so many blank walls, and only here and there a lace curtain waved out of the open window where some honest citizen was sleeping. The street was quite deserted; not even a cat or a policeman moved on it and Van Bibber's footsteps sounded brisk on the sidewalk. There was a great house at the corner of the avenue and the cross-street on which he was walking. The house faced the avenue and a stone wall ran back to the brown stone stable which opened on the side street. There was a door in this wall, and as

Van Bibber approached it on his solitary walk it opened cautiously, and a man's head appeared in it for an instant and was withdrawn again like a flash, and the door snapped to. Van Bibber stopped and looked at the door and at the house and up and down the street. The house was tightly closed, as though some one was lying inside dead, and the streets were still empty.

Van Bibber could think of nothing in his appearance so dreadful as to frighten an honest man, so he decided the face he had had a glimpse of must belong to a dishonest one. It was none of his business, he assured himself, but it was curious, and he liked adventure, and he would have liked to prove his friend the reporter, who did not believe in adventure, in the wrong. So he approached the door silently, and jumped and caught at the top of the wall and stuck one foot on the handle of the door, and, with the other on the knocker, drew himself up and looked cautiously down on the other side. He had done this so lightly that the only noise he made was the rattle of the door-knob on which his foot had rested, and the man inside thought that the one outside was trying to open the door, and placed his shoulder to it and pressed against it heavily. Van Bibber, from his perch on the top of the wall, looked down directly on the other's head and shoulders. He could see the top of the man's head only two feet below, and he also saw that in one hand he held a revolver and that two bags filled with projecting articles of different sizes lay at his feet.

It did not need explanatory notes to tell Van Bibber that the man below had robbed the big house on the corner, and that if it had not been for his having passed when he did the burglar would have escaped with his treasure. His first thought was that he was not a policeman, and that a fight with a burglar was not in his line of life; and this was followed by the thought that though the gentleman who owned the property in the two bags was of no interest to him, he was, as a respectable member of society, more entitled to consideration than the man with the revolver.

The fact that he was now, whether he liked it or not, perched on the top of the wall like Humpty Dumpty, and that the burglar might see him and shoot him the next minute, had also an immediate influence on his movements. So he balanced himself cautiously and noiselessly and dropped upon the man's head and shoulders, bringing him down to the flagged walk with him and under him. The revolver went off once in the struggle, but before the burglar could know how or from where his assailant had come, Van Bibber was standing up over him and had driven his heel down on his hand and kicked the pistol out of his fingers. Then he stepped quickly to where it lay and picked it up and said, "Now, if you try to get up I'll shoot at you." He felt an unwarranted and ill-timedly humorous inclination to add, "and I'll probably miss you," but subdued it. The burglar, much to Van Bibber's astonishment, did not attempt to rise, but sat up with his hands locked across his knees and said: "Shoot ahead. I'd a damned sight rather you would."

His teeth were set and his face desperate and bitter, and hopeless to a degree of utter hopelessness that Van Bibber had never imagined.

"Go ahead," reiterated the man, doggedly, "I won't move. Shoot me."

It was a most unpleasant situation. Van Bibber felt the

pistol loosening in his hand, and he was conscious of a strong inclination to lay it down and ask the burglar to tell him all about it.

"You haven't got much heart," said Van Bibber, finally. "You're a pretty poor sort of a burglar, I should say."

"What's the use?" said the man, fiercely. "I won't go back - I won't go back there alive. I've served my time forever in that hole. If I have to go back again - s'help me if I don't do for a keeper and die for it. But I won't serve there no more."

"Go back where?" asked Van Bibber, gently, and greatly interested; "to prison?"

"To prison, yes!" cried the man, hoarsely: "to a grave. That's where. Look at my face," he said, "and look at my hair. That ought to tell you where I've been. With all the color gone out of my skin, and all the life out of my legs. You needn't be afraid of me. I couldn't hurt you if I wanted to. I'm a skeleton and a baby, I am. I couldn't kill a cat. And now you're going to send me back again for another lifetime. For twenty years, this time, into that cold, forsaken hole, and after I done my time so well and worked so hard." Van Bibber shifted the pistol from one hand to the other and eyed his prisoner doubtfully.

"How long have you been out?" he asked, seating himself on the steps of the kitchen and holding the revolver between his knees. The sun was driving the morning mist away, and he had forgotten the cold.

"I got out yesterday," said the man.

Van Bibber glanced at the bags and lifted the revolver. "You didn't waste much time," he said.

"No," answered the man, sullenly, "no, I didn't. I knew this place and I wanted money to get West to my folks, and the Society said I'd have to wait until I earned it, and I couldn't wait. I haven't seen my wife for seven years, nor my daughter. Seven years, young man; think of that - seven years. Do you know how long that is? Seven years without seeing your wife or your child! And they're straight people, they are," he added, hastily. "My wife moved West after I was put away and took another name, and my girl never knew nothing about me. She thinks I'm away at sea. I was to join 'em. That was the plan. I was to join 'em, and I thought I could lift enough here to get the fare, and now," he added, dropping his face in his hands, "I've got to go back. And I had meant to live straight after I got West, - God help me, but I did! Not that it makes much difference now. An' I don't care whether you believe it or not neither," he added, fiercely.

"I didn't say whether I believed it or not," answered Van Bibber, with grave consideration.

He eyed the man for a brief space without speaking, and the burglar looked back at him, doggedly and defiantly, and with not the faintest suggestion of hope in his eyes, or of appeal for mercy. Perhaps it was because of this fact, or perhaps it was the wife and child that moved Van Bibber, but whatever his motives were, he acted on them promptly. "I suppose, though," he said, as though speaking to himself, "that I ought to give you up."

"I'll never go back alive," said the burglar, quietly.

"Well, that's bad, too," said Van Bibber. "Of course I don't know whether you're lying or not, and as to your meaning to live honestly, I very much doubt it; but I'll give you a ticket to wherever your wife is, and I'll see you on the train. And you can get off at the next station and rob my house to-morrow night, if you feel that way about it. Throw those bags inside that door where the servant will see them before the milkman does, and walk on out ahead of me, and keep your hands in your pockets, and don't try to run. I have your pistol, you know."

The man placed the bags inside the kitchen door; and, with a doubtful look at his custodian, stepped out into the street, and walked, as he was directed to do, toward the Grand Central station. Van Bibber kept just behind him, and kept turning the question over in his mind as to what he ought to do. He felt very guilty as he passed each policeman, but he recovered himself when he thought of the wife and child who lived in the West, and who were "straight."

"Where to?" asked Van Bibber, as he stood at the ticket-office window. "Helena, Montana," answered the man with, for the first time, a look of relief. Van Bibber bought the ticket and handed it to the burglar. "I suppose you know," he said, "that you can sell that at a place down town for half the money." "Yes, I know that," said the burglar. There was a half-hour before the train left, and Van Bibber took his charge into the restaurant and watched him eat everything placed before him, with his eyes glancing all the while to the right or left. Then Van Bibber gave him some money and told him to write to him, and shook hands with him. The man nodded eagerly and pulled off his hat as the car drew out of the station; and Van Bibber came down town again with the shop girls and clerks going to work, still wondering if he had done the right thing.

He went to his rooms and changed his clothes, took a cold bath, and crossed over to Delmonico's for his breakfast, and, while the waiter laid the cloth in the cafe, glanced at the headings in one of the papers. He scanned first with polite interest the account of the dance on the night previous and noticed his name among those present. With greater interest he read of the fight between "Dutchy" Mack and the "Black Diamond," and then he read carefully how "Abe" Hubbard, alias "Jimmie the Gent," a burglar, had broken jail in New Jersey, and had been traced to New York. There was a description of the man, and Van Bibber breathed quickly as he read it. "The detectives have a clew of his whereabouts," the account said; "if he is still in the city they are confident of recapturing him. But they fear that the same friends who helped him to break jail will probably assist him from the country or to get out West."

"They may do that," murmured Van Bibber to himself, with a smile of grim contentment; "they probably will."

Then he said to the waiter, "Oh, I don't know. Some bacon and eggs and green things and coffee."

VAN BIBBER AS BEST MAN

Young Van Bibber came up to town in June from Newport to see his lawyer about the preparation of some papers that needed his signature. He found the city very hot and close, and as dreary and as empty as a house that has been shut up for some time while its usual occupants are away in the country.

As he had to wait over for an afternoon train, and as he was down town, he decided to lunch at a French restaurant near Washington Square, where some one had told him you could get particular things particularly well cooked. The tables were set on a terrace with plants and flowers about them, and covered with a tricolored awning. There were no jangling horse-car bells nor dust to disturb him, and almost all the other tables were unoccupied. The waiters leaned against these tables and chatted in a French argot; and a cool breeze blew through the plants and billowed the awning, so that, on the whole, Van Bibber was glad he had come.

There was, beside himself, an old Frenchman scolding over his late breakfast; two young artists with Van Dyke beards, who ordered the most remarkable things in the same French argot that the waiters spoke; and a young lady and a young gentleman at the table next to his own. The young man's back was toward him, and he could only see the girl when the youth moved to one side. She was very young and very pretty, and she seemed in a most excited state of mind from the tip of her wide-brimmed, pointed French hat to the points of her patent-leather ties. She was strikingly well-bred in appearance, and Van Bibber wondered why she should be dining alone with so young a man.

"It wasn't my fault," he heard the youth say earnestly. "How could I know he would be out of town? and anyway it really doesn't matter. Your cousin is not the only clergyman in the city."

"Of course not," said the girl, almost tearfully, "but they're not my cousins and he is, and that would have made it so much, oh, so very much different. I'm awfully frightened!"

"Runaway couple," commented Van Bibber. "Most interesting. Read about 'em often; never seen 'em. Most interesting."

He bent his head over an entree, but he could not help hearing what followed, for the young runaways were indifferent to all around them, and though he rattled his knife and fork in a most vulgar manner, they did not heed him nor lower their voices.

"Well, what are you going to do?" said the girl, severely but not unkindly. "It doesn't seem to me that you are exactly rising to the occasion."

"Well, I don't know," answered the youth, easily. "We're safe here anyway. Nobody we know ever comes here, and if they did they are out of town now. You go on and eat something, and I'll get a directory and look up a lot of clergymen's addresses, and then we can make out a list and drive around in a cab until we find one who has not gone off on his vacation. We ought to be able to catch the Fall River boat back at five this afternoon; then we can go right on to Boston from Fall River to-morrow morning and run down to Narragansett during the day."

"They'll never forgive us," said the girl.

"Oh, well, that's all right," exclaimed the young man, cheerfully. "Really, you're the most uncomfortable young person I ever ran away with. One might think you were going to a funeral. You were willing enough two days ago, and now you don't help me at all. Are you sorry?" he asked, and then added, "but please don't say so, even if you are."

"No, not sorry, exactly," said the girl; "but, indeed, Ted, it is going to make so much talk. If we only had a girl with us, or if you had a best man, or if we had witnesses, as they do in England, and a parish registry, or something of that sort; or if Cousin Harold had only been at home to do the marrying."

The young gentleman called Ted did not look, judging from the expression of his shoulders, as if he were having a very good time.

He picked at the food on his plate gloomily, and the girl took out her handkerchief and then put it resolutely back again and smiled at him. The youth called the waiter and told him to bring a directory, and as he turned to give the order Van Bibber recognized him and he recognized Van Bibber. Van Bibber knew him for a very nice boy, of a very good Boston family named Standish, and the younger of two sons. It was the elder who was Van Bibber's particular friend. The girl saw nothing of this mutual recognition, for she was looking with startled eyes at a hansom that had dashed up the side street and was turning the corner.

"Ted, O Ted!" she gasped. "It's your brother. There! In that hansom. I saw him perfectly plainly. Oh, how did he find us? What shall we do?"

Ted grew very red and then very white.

"Standish," said Van Bibber, jumping up and reaching for his hat, "pay this chap for these things, will you, and I'll get rid of your brother."

Van Bibber descended the steps lighting a cigar as the elder Standish came up them on a jump.

"Hello, Standish!" shouted the New Yorker. "Wait a minute; where are you going? Why, it seems to rain Standishes to-day! First see your brother; then I see you. What's on?"

"You've seen him?" cried the Boston man, eagerly. "Yes, and where is he? Was she with him? Are they married? Am I in time?"

Van Bibber answered these different questions to the effect that he had seen young Standish and Mrs. Standish not a half an hour before, and that they were just then taking a cab for Jersey City, whence they were to depart for Chicago.

"The driver who brought them here, and who told me where they were, said they could not have left this place by the time I would reach it," said the elder brother, doubtfully.

"That's so," said the driver of the cab, who had listened curiously. "I brought 'em here not more'n half an hour ago. Just had time to get back to the depot. They can't have gone long."

"Yes, but they have," said Van Bibber. "However, if you get over to Jersey City in time for the 2.30, you can reach Chicago almost as soon as they do. They are going to the Palmer House, they said."

"Thank you, old fellow," shouted Standish, jumping back into his hansom. "It's a terrible business. Pair of young fools. Nobody objected to the marriage, only too young, you know. Ever so much obliged."

"Don't mention it," said Van Bibber, politely.

"Now, then," said that young man, as he approached the frightened couple trembling on the terrace, "I've sent your brother off to Chicago. I do not know why I selected Chicago as a place where one would go on a honeymoon. But I'm not used to lying and I'm not very good at it. Now, if you will introduce me, I'll see what can be done toward getting you two babes out of the woods."

Standish said, "Miss Cambridge, this is Mr. Cortlandt Van Bibber, of whom you have heard my brother speak," and Miss Cambridge said she was very glad to meet Mr. Van Bibber even under such peculiarly trying circumstances.

"Now what you two want to do," said Van Bibber,

addressing them as though they were just about fifteen years old and he were at least forty, "is to give this thing all the publicity you can."

"What?" chorused the two runaways, in violent protest.

"Certainly," said Van Bibber. "You were about to make a fatal mistake. You were about to go to some unknown clergyman of an unknown parish, who would have married you in a back room, without a certificate or a witness, just like any eloping farmer's daughter and lightning-rod agent. Now it's different with you two. Why you were not married respectably in church I don't know, and I do not intend to ask, but a kind Providence has sent me to you to see that there is no talk nor scandal, which is such bad form, and which would have got your names into all the papers. I am going to arrange this wedding properly, and you will kindly remain here until I send a carriage for you. Now just rely on me entirely and eat your luncheon in peace. It's all going to come out right - and allow me to recommend the salad, which is especially good."

Van Bibber first drove madly to the Little Church Around the Corner, where he told the kind old rector all about it, and arranged to have the church open and the assistant organist in her place, and a district-messenger boy to blow the bellows, punctually at three o'clock. "And now," he soliloquized, "I must get some names. It doesn't matter much whether they happen to know the high contracting parties or not, but they must be names that everybody knows. Whoever is in town will be lunching at Delmonico's, and the men will be at the clubs." So he first went to the big restaurant, where, as good luck would have it, he found Mrs. "Regy" Van Arnt and Mrs. "Jack" Peabody, and the

Misses Brookline, who had run up the Sound for the day on the yacht *Minerva* of the Boston Yacht Club, and he told them how things were and swore them to secrecy, and told them to bring what men they could pick up.

At the club he pressed four men into service who knew everybody and whom everybody knew, and when they protested that they had not been properly invited and that they only knew the bride and groom by sight, he told them that made no difference, as it was only their names he wanted. Then he sent a messenger boy to get the biggest suit of rooms on the Fall River boat and another one for flowers, and then he put Mrs. "Regy" Van Arnt into a cab and sent her after the bride, and, as best man, he got into another cab and carried off the groom.

"I have acted either as best man or usher forty-two times now," said Van Bibber, as they drove to the church, "and this is the first time I ever appeared in either capacity in russia-leather shoes and a blue serge yachting suit. But then," he added, contentedly, "you ought to see the other fellows. One of them is in a striped flannel."

Mrs. "Regy" and Miss Cambridge wept a great deal on the way up town, but the bride was smiling and happy when she walked up the aisle to meet her prospective husband, who looked exceedingly conscious before the eyes of the men, all of whom he knew by sight or by name, and not one of whom he had ever met before. But they all shook hands after it was over, and the assistant organist played the Wedding March, and one of the club men insisted in pulling a cheerful and jerky peal on the church bell in the absence of the janitor, and then Van Bibber hurled an old shoe and a handful of rice - which he had thoughtfully collected from the chef at the club - after them as they drove off to the boat.

"Now," said Van Bibber, with a proud sigh of relief and satisfaction, "I will send that to the papers, and when it is printed to-morrow it will read like one of the most orthodox and one of the smartest weddings of the season. And yet I can't help thinking -"

"Well?" said Mrs. "Regy," as he paused doubtfully.

"Well, I can't help thinking," continued Van Bibber, "of Standish's older brother racing around Chicago with the thermometer at 102 in the shade. I wish I had only sent him to Jersey City. It just shows," he added, mournfully, "that when a man is not practised in lying, he should leave it alone."

Choose from Thousands of 1stWorldLibrary Classics By

A. M. Barnard
Ada Leverson
Adolphus William Ward
Aesop
Agatha Christie
Alexander Aaronsohn
Alexander Kielland
Alexandre Dumas
Alfred Gatty
Alfred Ollivant
Alice Duer Miller
Alice Turner Curtis
Alice Dunbar
Ambrose Bierce
Amelia E. Barr
Amory H. Bradford
Andrew Lang
Andrew McFarland Davis
Andy Adams
Anna Sewell
Annie Besant
Annie Hamilton Donnell
Annie Payson Call
Annonaymous
Anton Chekhov
Arnold Bennett
Arthur Conan Doyle
Arthur M. Winfield
Arthur Ransome
Atticus
B.H. Baden-Powell
B. M. Bower
Baroness Emmuska Orczy
Baroness Orczy
Basil King
Bayard Taylor
Ben Macomber
Bertha Muzzy Bower
Bjornstjerne Bjornson
Booth Tarkington
Boyd Cable
Bram Stoker
C. Collodi
C. E. Orr
C. M. Ingleby
Carolyn Wells
Catherine Parr Traill
Charles A. Eastman
Charles Dickens

Charles Dudley Warner
Charles Farrar Browne
Charles Ives
Charles Kingsley
Charles Klein
Charles Amory Beach
Charles Hanson Towne
Charles Lathrop Pack
Charles Whibley
Charles Willing Beale
Charlotte M. Braeme
Charlotte M. Yonge
Charlotte Perkins Stetson
Clair W. Hayes
Clarence Day Jr.
Clarence E. Mulford
Clemence Housman
Confucius
Cornelis DeWitt Wilcox
Cyril Burleigh
D. H. Lawrence
Daniel Defoe
David Garnett
Dinah Craik
Don Carlos Janes
Donald Keyhoe
Dorothy Kilner
Dougan Clark
Douglas Fairbanks
E. Nesbit
E.P.Roe
E. Phillips Oppenheim
Earl Barnes
Edgar Rice Burroughs
Edith Van Dyne
Edith Wharton
Edward J. O'Biren
Edward S. Ellis
Edwin L. Arnold
Eleanor Atkins
Eliot Gregory
Elizabeth Gaskell
Elizabeth McCracken
Elizabeth Von Arnim
Ellem Key
Emerson Hough
Emilie F. Carlen
Emily Dickinson
Enid Bagnold

Enilor Macartney Lane
Erasmus W. Jones
Ernie Howard Pie
Ethel Turner
Ethel Watts Mumford
Eugenie Foa
Eugene Wood
Eustace Hale Ball
Evelyn Everett-green
Everard Cotes
F. H. Cheley
F. J. Cross
Federick Austin Ogg
Ferdinand Ossendowski
Francis Bacon
Francis Darwin
Frances Hodgson Burnett
Frances Parkinson Keyes
Frank Gee Patchin
Frank Harris
Frank Jewett Mather
Frank L. Packard
Frank V. Webster
Frederic Stewart Isham
Frederick Trevor Hill
Frederick Winslow Taylor
Friedrich Kerst
Friedrich Nietzsche
Fyodor Dostoyevsky
G.A. Henty
G.K. Chesterton
Gabrielle E. Jackson
Garrett P. Serviss
Gaston Leroux
George A. Warren
George Ade
Geroge Bernard Shaw
George Durston
George Ebers
George Eliot
George Gissing
George MacDonald
George Meredith
George Orwell
George Sylvester Viereck
George Tucker
George W. Cable
George Wharton James
Gertrude Atherton

Grace E. King
Grace Gallatin
Grant Allen
Guillermo A. Sherwell
Gulielma Zollinger
Gustav Flaubert
H. A. Cody
H. B. Irving
H.C. Bailey
H. G. Wells
H. H. Munro
H. Irving Hancock
H. Rider Haggard
H. W. C. Davis
Hamilton Wright Mabie
Hans Christian Andersen
Harold Avery
Harold McGrath
Harriet Beecher Stowe
Harry Houidini
Helent Hunt Jackson
Helen Nicolay
Hendrik Conscience
Hendy David Thoreau
Henri Barbusse
Henrik Ibsen
Henry Adams
Henry Ford
Henry Frost
Henry James
Henry Jones Ford
Henry Seton Merriman
Henry W Longfellow
Herbert A. Giles
Herbert N. Casson
Herman Hesse
Homer
Honore De Balzac
Horace Walpole
Horatio Alger Jr.
Howard Pyle
Howard R. Garis
Hugh Lofting
Hugh Walpole
Humphry Ward
Ian Maclaren
Inez Haynes Gillmore
Irving Bacheller
Israel Abrahams
Ivan Turgenev
J.G.Austin

J. Henri Fabre
J. M. Barrie
J. Macdonald Oxley
J. S. Fletcher
J. S. Knowles
J. Storer Clouston
Jack London
Jacob Abbott
James Allen
James Andrews
James Baldwin
James DeMille
James Joyce
James Lane Allen
James Lane Allen
James Oliver Curwood
James Oppenheim
James Otis
James R. Driscoll
Jane Austen
Janet Aldridge
Jens Peter Jacobsen
Jerome K. Jerome
John Burroughs
John Cournos
John F. Kennedy
John Gay
John Glasworthy
John Habberton
John Joy Bell
John Kendrick Bangs
John Milton
John Philip Sousa
Jonas Lauritz Idemil Lie
Jonathan Swift
Joseph A. Altsheler
Joseph Carey
Joseph Conrad
Joseph E. Badger Jr
Joseph Hergesheimer
Joseph Jacobs
Jules Vernes
Julian Hawthrone
Julie A Lippmann
Justin Huntly McCarthy
Kakuzo Okakura
Kenneth Grahame
Kenneth McGaffey
Kate Langley Bosher
Kate Langley Bosher
Katherine Cecil Thurston

Katherine Stokes
L. A. Abbot
L. T. Meade
L. Frank Baum
Latta Griswold
Laura Lee Hope
Laurence Housman
Lawrence Beasley
Leo Tolstoy
Leonid Andreyev
Lewis Carroll
Lewis Sperry Chafer
Lilian Bell
Lloyd Osbourne
Louis Hughes
Louis Tracy
Louisa May Alcott
Lucy Fitch Perkins
Lucy Maud Montgomery
Lydia Miller Middleton
Lyndon Orr
M. Corvus
M. H. Adams
Margaret E. Sangster
Margaret Vandercook
Margret Penrose
Maria Edgeworth
Maria Thompson Daviess
Mariano Azuela
Marion Polk Angellotti
Mark Overton
Mark Twain
Mary Austin
Mary Catherine Crowley
Mary Cole
Mary Hastings Bradley
Mary Roberts Rinehart
Mary Rowlandson
M. Wollstonecraft Shelley
Maud Lindsay
Max Beerbohm
Myra Kelly
Nathaniel Hawthrone
Nicolo Machiavelli
O. F. Walton
Oscar Wilde
Owen Johnson
P.G. Wodehouse
Paul and Mabel Thorne
Paul G. Tomlinson
Paul Severing

Percy Brebner
Peter B. Kyne
Plato
R. Derby Holmes
R. L. Stevenson
R. S. Ball
Rabindranath Tagore
Rahul Alvares
Ralph Bonehill
Ralph Henry Barbour
Ralph Victor
Ralph Waldo Emmerson
Rene Descartes
Rex Beach
Rex E. Beach
Richard Harding Davis
Richard Jefferies
Richard Le Gallienne
Robert Barr
Robert Frost
Robert Gordon Anderson
Robert L. Drake
Robert Lansing
Robert Lynd
Robert Michael Ballantyne
Robert W. Chambers
Rosa Nouchette Carey
Rudyard Kipling
Samuel B. Allison

Samuel Hopkins Adams
Sarah Bernhardt
Sarah C. Hallowell
Selma Lagerlof
Sherwood Anderson
Sigmund Freud
Standish O'Grady
Stanley Weyman
Stella Benson
Stephen Crane
Stewart Edward White
Stijn Streuvels
Swami Abhedananda
Swami Parmananda
T. S. Ackland
T. S. Arthur
The Princess Der Ling
Thomas A. Janvier
Thomas A Kempis
Thomas Anderton
Thomas Bailey Aldrich
Thomas Bulfinch
Thomas De Quincey
Thomas H. Huxley
Thomas Hardy
Thomas More
Thornton W. Burgess
U. S. Grant
Valentine Williams

Various Authors
Vaughan Kester
Victor Appleton
Virginia Woolf
Walter Camp
Walter Scott
Washington Irving
Wilbur Lawton
Wilkie Collins
Willa Cather
Willard F. Baker
William Dean Howells
William le Queux
W. Makepeace Thackeray
William W. Walter
Winston Churchill
Yei Theodora Ozaki
Yogi Ramacharaka
Young E. Allison
Zane Grey